"Not bothering to say goodbye, Sarah?"

There was so much sarcasm in his voice, so much unexpected criticism and condemnation of her manner of leaving.

"I...I didn't want to disturb you," she told him nervously.

"No, I'm sure you didn't."

He was looking at her, studying her, and for some reason, her embarrassment changed to a suffocating, acute awareness of him. Something had touched a deeply rooted sensual chord within her, so that her whole body seemed to vibrate in response to awareness of him.

Still looking at her, he said silkily, "What a pity you didn't think about *that* before, isn't it?"

PENNY JORDAN was constantly in trouble in school because of her inability to stop daydreaming—especially during French lessons. In her teens, she was an avid romance reader, although it didn't occur to her to try writing one herself until she was older. "My first half-dozen attempts ended up ingloriously," she remembers, "but I persevered, and one manuscript was finished." She plucked up the courage to send it to a publisher, convinced her book would be rejected. It wasn't, and the rest is history! Penny is married and lives in Cheshire.

Penny Jordan's striking mainstream novel *Power Play* quickly became a *New York Times* bestseller. She followed that success with *Silver*, *The Hidden Years*, and *Lingering Shadows*.

Don't miss Penny's latest blockbuster, *For Better For Worse*, available in December.

Books by Penny Jordan

HARLEQUIN PRESENTS
1544—DANGEROUS INTERLOPER
1552—SECOND-BEST HUSBAND
1625—MISTAKEN ADVERSARY

HARLEQUIN PRESENTS PLUS
1575—A CURE FOR LOVE
1599—STRANGER FROM THE PAST
1655—PAST PASSION

Don't miss any of our special offers. Write to us at the following address for information on our newest releases.

Harlequin Reader Service
U.S.: 3010 Walden Ave., P.O. Box 1325, Buffalo, NY 14269
Canadian: P.O. Box 609, Fort Erie, Ont. L2A 5X3

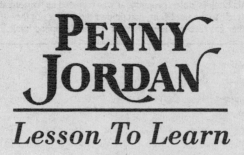

PENNY JORDAN

Lesson To Learn

Harlequin Books

TORONTO • NEW YORK • LONDON
AMSTERDAM • PARIS • SYDNEY • HAMBURG
STOCKHOLM • ATHENS • TOKYO • MILAN
MADRID • WARSAW • BUDAPEST • AUCKLAND

ISBN 0-373-11673-X

LESSON TO LEARN

CHAPTER ONE

SARAH settled herself comfortably against the trunk of the willow and closed her eyes. Letting the soft gurgle of the stream gently lull her towards sleep, she firmly ignored the pangs of guilt trying to remind her that she was supposed to be thinking about her future; about her superiors' concern that because of her lack of detachment, her apparent inability to stop herself from becoming emotionally involved with her pupils, she was seriously hindering her career as a teacher.

Ignoring the niggling reminder that her cousin had given her this morning, that sleep could sometimes be used as an anodyne against depression, she told herself that it was as a result of the stress of the recently ended term that she felt so exhausted, so drained, so completely unable to take charge of her life and direct it firmly back into the ambitious channels she had planned for herself during her time at university.

Then it had all seemed so simple: she would get her degree, she would go into teaching; she would progress up her career ladder, perhaps even moving into the private sector for a while before applying for the challenging position of head teacher, and she would attain that goal before her thirtieth birthday.

And yet here she was at twenty-seven, acknowledging—or, rather, being forced to acknowledge—

that in her original formula for her career she had neglected to take into account one vital factor, namely that she would become so involved with her pupils, so concerned for them, that her own needs, her own plans, her own life, would become completely submerged in her desire to help them.

Exhaustion was how her doctor had sympathetically described the intense physical and mental weakness which had overtaken her midway through last term; stress—the stress of modern living and of a job that made far too many demands upon her.

Her superiors had confirmed that diagnosis, but had been less sympathetic, telling her that her problems were self-inflicted; pointing out that no one had asked her to take on the extra responsibility of organising out-of-school activities for the twelve-year-olds in her care; that no one but herself was to blame for the fact that she seemed to have no defences against taking her pupils and their problems to her heart and suffering with them.

The enormous comprehensive where she worked had a far too rapid turnover of staff, quickly disillusioned by the problems caused by dealing with such vast numbers of children; the children themselves, many of them from disadvantaged backgrounds, were sometimes difficult to deal with, Sarah had to acknowledge that, but most of them, given time and encouragement, would respond...

She gave a small sigh. Forget about your job, her doctor had advised her. Take yourself off somewhere relaxing; lie in the sun... unwind...

Of course, that would have been impossible. Teachers did not spend the entire long summer

break without any work to do, as so many people
outside the profession seemed to believe, but then
had come the news that, even if she was not actually being formally suspended, her future as a
teacher was in grave doubt. Which was why she
had come here to Shropshire to stay with her cousin
and her husband in their quiet country village,
where Sally, her cousin, had promised her she would
find all the peace and relaxation she needed.

Ross and Sally had been married for two years;
Ross worked for an innovative engineering firm in
Ludlow, and Sally was an illustrator, working from
a small downstairs study in their pretty ex-
farmhouse.

Both of them had made Sarah welcome, but their
jobs meant that she was left very much to her own
devices during the day. Which was what she
wanted . . . or at least what her doctor had said she
needed. And it was true that since she had come
to Shropshire two weeks ago the problems of her
pupils, and the anxieties caused by her over-
involvement with them, were beginning to lessen
their grip on her, but even that was causing her to
feel guilt, to remind herself that they, unlike her,
were not fortunate enough to have kind cousins
living in idyllic country surroundings, so that they
too could escape from the enervating, choking heat
of a city simmering under a very un-English and
long-lasting heatwave.

On the news at night there were photographs of
parched dry fields and parks, of empty streams,
and city streets with melting tarmac, and hard blue
skies.

A small plopping sound from the stream caused her to open her eyes and focus on the fish jumping out of the water to catch flies. It was a fair-sized trout, and the sight of it made her smile, remembering childhood fishing trips with her father and brother.

Her parents were in Canada now, visiting John and Heather and their twin sons... which was why Sally's invitation had been such a godsend.

Sarah had always got on well with her cousin. Sally was her senior by three years and there had always been a bond between them. She had been chief bridesmaid at Sally and Ross's wedding two years ago, although it had been over a year since she had last seen them.

The shock Sally had tried to hide when she had met her from the train had been quickly followed by her cousin's verbally expressed concern over her loss of weight and the tension dulling her skin and her eyes.

When she had first arrived no one seeing them together would ever have believed that she was the younger, Sarah acknowledged, but now, as she gave in to her body's demand for rest and relaxation and tried to put aside her mental and emotional guilt at being so self-indulgent, she was slowly starting to regain some of the weight she had lost so that her five-foot frame looked more slender than gaunt, and her skin had begun to lose its city pallor and strain. That was the trouble with being a redhead: at times of emotional, physical or mental upset one's skin did tend to reflect those stresses and become so pale in contrast to one's hair that the effect was over-dramatic.

How the days she had spent outside had given her a warm peachy glow, and Ross had jokingly remarked over dinner the previous night, and Sally had commented as she was coming out this morning, that she was once again starting to look like the stunning sexy redhead who had generated so much male curiosity and comment at the wedding.

Sarah had pulled a face and grimaced at her. She personally would never have described herself as either sexy or stunning. She moved, trying not to recall the problems she had had when she had first entered teaching and some of her male colleagues, and even the older male pupils, had refused to take her seriously because of her looks. It was the combination of red hair and startlingly intense green eyes, plus the high cheekbones and pointed chin she had inherited from her mother, that was responsible for the unintentional sensuality of her looks.

In her teens those looks had caused her endless problems, often antagonising her own sex and making it difficult for her to make friends, and equally often leading the boys she met to assume that she was far more sexually aware and adventurous than was actually the case.

At university she had found that the best way to deal with the problem was to adopt a firm no-nonsense manner in such direct contrast to her looks that it immediately made it obvious that she was at university for the serious business of studying and obtaining her degree and not to have a good time.

By the time she had left university and started her first job she had learned to tuck her long hair

into a neat chignon, and to play down her facial
features by wearing only a minimum of make-up.
She always chose sensible, sturdy clothes, suppressing her own unruly and dangerous urge to wear
something more feminine and appealing.

Sally had grimaced with distaste when she had
met her from the train, immediately condemning
the beige shirtwaister dress she was wearing as un-
believably frumpy and sexless.

Sarah had started to point out that, as a teacher,
the last thing she wanted was to be regarded as sexually provocative, but she had been too exhausted,
too drained, to bother. Just as she had been unable
to find the energy to resist when Sally had dragged
her off to Ludlow and ruthlessly insisted on replacing almost everything in the sparse wardrobe
she had brought with her.

Which was why today she was dressed in a skimpy
halter-necked white top and a pair of cut-off denim
jeans, her bare feet thrust into a pair of trainers,
her hair caught up on top of her head in an untidy
pony-tail to keep it off the back of her neck.

This heatwave was so enervating. It was an effort
to think, never mind to move, or was it more because she was so exhausted that it seemed so much
simpler to let others direct the course of her life,
to simply give in and let herself go with the flow?

Behind her, upstream, a small creature disturbed
by the passage of someone along the path made a
noise that set the birds off in sharp shrill cries of
warning.

Immediately Sarah felt her own muscles tense in
response. This path was so quiet that she had almost
begun to think of it as her own private retreat. As

she drew herself further into the protection of the willow's overhanging branches she hoped that whoever was coming towards her would walk past her without stopping to chat.

It was a new experience for her, this reluctance to involve herself with anyone. A result, perhaps, of the lecture she had received from her superiors when they had warned her that her over-involvement with her pupils was detrimental to her career.

She closed her eyes, determinedly blotting out the sound of someone approaching her hiding-place, but it was impossible to ignore the timid and very youthful voice that said uncertainly and very anxiously, 'Excuse me, but is this the right way to Ludlow?'

Unwillingly she opened her eyes.

A child...a boy, no more than six years old at most, was standing watching her. He was fair-haired and blue-eyed, a little too thin for his age and with an anxiety about him that her senses quickly regis-tered and recognised.

Even while she was telling herself that, whoever he was and whatever he was doing here all on his own on this remote country footpath, it was nothing to do with her, and that all she had to do was to answer his question and set him on his way, another part of her, that compassionate, caring, womanly part of her that had already caused her so many problems was wondering who he was, and why he was here, so very, very much alone, and so very, very young.

As she sat up and studied him she fibbed, 'I don't really know, but I've got a map somewhere here

with me...if you'd like to come and sit down for
a moment I'll have a look at it.'

That was true at any rate, she did have a map,
and she also had the very generous lunch that Mrs
Beattie, Sally's wonderful daily, had packed up for
her that morning.

Reluctantly the child took a step towards her,
looking backwards over his shoulder as he did so.
Now there was fear in his eyes as well as tension.

What was he running away from? Sarah wondered as she deliberately, very slowly opened the
rucksack beside her, and equally deliberately, with
nonchalant casualness, removed a can of soft drink
and some sandwiches. The child was betraying his
youth by his very lack of preparation for his
odyssey. His clothes, too, seemed to have been
chosen without much regard for their practi-
cality—a pair of heavy jeans, a T-shirt, and on his
feet what looked like a pair of baseball boots. The
jeans were far too hot and heavy for this weather
and they were also too big for him. His T-shirt and
his boots, though, were obviously expensive, which
ruled out the jeans having been bought with extra
growing-room...which seemed to suggest that
whoever had bought them had not really been sure
of his size.

A tiny frown touched her forehead as Sarah deliberately took her time over extricating the map
from the rucksack.

Pretending to be unaware of his tension and the
anxious way he kept on looking back in the direction he had just come, she patted the ground
beside her, and said easily, 'Come and sit down.
I'm afraid I'm not very good with maps, so it may

take me quite a while to find out if you're on the right path. I'm only on holiday here, you see. What about you? Do you live round here?'

She watched him as he automatically started to respond to her question and then caught himself up after he had started to say, 'Yes. I live...' his face suddenly settling into stubborn unhappy lines. 'I'm staying here,' he told her gruffly. 'But I don't really live here.'

'Ah.'

Sarah unfolded the map, and then, although she herself was not particularly hungry, she unwrapped some of Mrs Beattie's sandwiches and started to eat one, pausing to indicate the open foil-wrapped package and to say, 'Would you like a sandwich?'

He nodded his head, and then said huskily, 'Yes, please. I am rather hungry.'

He had excellent manners; his speech was almost old-fashionedly formal, as though he had spent a long time with older people. Thoughtfully Sarah watched him as he devoured his sandwich.

She knew already that she would not let him go; that she would have to somehow or other win his confidence and then restore him to his family.

A child of his age on his own . . . there were so many hazards . . . so many dangers, from man as well as from nature. His family, whoever they were and wherever they lived, must be going frantic with worry if they knew that he was missing.

She suspected he had not come very far and that the exhaustion she could see so clearly in his eyes came more from misery and fear than from the physical effort of having walked a long way.

He had a scratch on one arm where he had obviously pushed past a bramble, and there were smears of dirt on his T-shirt. He had finished his sandwich and was eyeing the others in the pile with a hungry intensity that made Sarah hide a small smile as she offered casually, 'Finished? Have another?'

'You know,' she told him as he bit eagerly into the bread, 'I'm not sure that you are on the right path. From this map, it looks as though...' She paused, frowning, ignoring the tension she could feel emanating from him. 'I think you could possibly pick up the path half a mile or so further on.'

'Half a mile; is that a very long way?'

'Fairly... and then it's another six or seven miles to Ludlow. Are you going there for something important?'

As she looked at him she saw that he was avoiding her eyes, not wanting to lie to her, but obviously not wanting to tell her the truth either.

'Never mind... there might be a short cut,' she offered, re-studying the map. 'It's a pity I don't have a car, otherwise I could drive you there.'

She paused to see how he was going to react to this suggestion, and was relieved to see hesitance and reluctance.

'I'm not allowed to go in cars with strangers,' he told her immediately.

Sarah suppressed a small sigh. Poor kid, hadn't anyone warned him that talking to strangers could be equally dangerous?

'No, of course not,' she agreed gravely, investigating the rucksack and offering him an apple. He was still standing up and she patted the ground beside her again and invited, 'If you come and sit down here you can have a look at the map. I'm not very good at reading them.'

'No...my mother isn't either...' He broke off, his expression suddenly changing. 'I mean...she wasn't.'

He had turned his head, tucking it into his shoulder defensively, a betraying tremor wobbling his voice.

Was his mother no longer alive, as his words seemed to imply, or was she merely no longer a part of his life? Sarah was in no doubt now that he was running away and that he was desperately unhappy, but he was still obeying her suggestion and coming to sit down beside her.

He was old enough to have left his baby-fat behind him, but his arms and legs still had the softness of early childhood, and as he sat down beside her he smelled of clean young skin and sunshine.

'My name's Sarah...what's yours?' she asked him as she moved the map so that he could look at it.

'Robert,' he told her, 'although...'

'Robert...that's a very grown-up name,' Sarah admired. 'Doesn't anyone call you Bobbie?'

He shook his head.

'My...my...Nana used to call me Robbie, but he said it was a baby's name. He calls me Robert.' His face suddenly crumpled up, tears shimmering in his eyes, and Sarah respected that the 'he' referred to with such anger and dislike was most probably his father.

Unwilling to probe too much and to frighten him into silence before she had obtained from him the information she needed, she didn't push him but said simply and pacifically, 'Well, Robert is a very grown-up name, and I expect you must be...well, at least eight.'

She could see the way her words caused his chest to swell with pride and his tears to disappear.

'I'm six,' he told her. 'Almost seven. Well, I'll be seven in May.'

In May. It was only July now, which meant that he was in fact only just six, but Sarah widened her eyes admiringly and commented that she had thought he was much, much older.

'Won't your...your nana be missing you, though, Robert?' she suggested gently. 'She'll be wondering where you are, I'm sure. Did you leave her a note?'

Immediately his eyes filled with tears as he shook his head and burst out, 'Nana's dead. She died in a car accident with my mother and Tom...and I had to come back here and live with...with him. I hate him. I want to go back home. I don't want to stay with him any more. Mrs Richards could look after me. She did before when my mother and Tom were away and Nana was ill. I don't have to stay here with him. My mother told me that. She said I didn't have to see him if I didn't want to and I didn't want to. I don't like him. My mother said he'd never wanted me anyway...that he only wanted me to get at her.'

As she listened to the jumbled staccato words Sarah fought down the wave of compassion making her own eyes moisten and her heart ache.

From what he wasn't saying as much as from
what he was, she was beginning to build up a clear
picture of what must have happened. His parents
were either separated or divorced; he had obviously
lived with his mother and perhaps his grandmother
as well in some other part of the country, and from
what he had said it sounded as though he had lost
them in a car accident and was now living with his
father. A father who, it seemed, had never wanted
him and who had perhaps only reluctantly accepted responsibility for him now. Poor child, no
wonder he was so unhappy, no wonder he was
running away, but, much as her heart ached for
him, much as she sympathised with him, she had
to find a way of discovering where he lived and
who his father was.

'So you're going to find Mrs Richards, is that
it?' she hazarded, causing him to nod his head.
'Where does she live? Is it far away?'

'She lives in London,' he told her importantly.

'London; that's a long way to go,' Sarah commented sympathetically. 'A very long way. Have
you been walking for a long time?'

'I left after breakfast,' he told her immediately
and innocently, causing Sarah a panic of guilt for
the way she was deceiving him. But it was for his
own good...his own protection. 'I had to wait until
he...my father had gone to work. Mrs Jacobs went
out shopping. She told me not to go out of the
garden. I don't like her.'

Mrs Jacobs. Sarah bit her bottom lip. Surely she
had heard Mrs Beattie mentioning a Mrs Jacobs
who was one of her neighbours in the village? She
had gained the impression that the two women were

not good friends and that Sally's cleaner heartily despised and disliked the other woman.

'Did ... did you leave your father a note?' Sarah asked him.

He shook his head, his face settling into a stubborn mask.

'He won't care. He'll be glad to see the back of me,' he told her. 'Mrs Jacobs says I'm a nuisance and that I cause too much dis ... dis ...'

'Disruption?' Sarah suggested. She suppressed a sigh as he nodded his head, plainly impressed by her mind-reading abilities. Much as she sympathised with him, she was going to have to get his address out of him and take him home.

Unpleasant though both Mrs Jacobs and his father sounded, she could see no obvious signs of any kind of physical or emotional abuse about him, and she was experienced enough to have recognised them had they been there. For all his fear and apprehension, he lacked the desperate silence, the smell of fear that seemed to emanate from such children.

But he *was* unhappy, desperately so, and she could not help wondering a little about his father, questioning what manner of man he was. She had the impression from what Robert had told her that his father saw him as a burden ... a nuisance.

'And that's why you're going to London ... to find Mrs Richards.'

'I'd rather live with her than with my father,' Robert told her, tears filling his eyes as he repeated, 'I don't like him.'

Instinctively Sarah opened her arms to him, and he ran into them, his small body shaken by sobs as she held him, soothing him, comforting him. Poor baby, and he was still only a baby, for all his attempts to pretend otherwise.

Soon, when he had calmed down a little, she would try to coax him into agreeing to go home, but for the moment it was more important to win his confidence and comfort him than to question him, and so she let him cry, gently rocking him, while she smoothed his fair hair.

Absorbed in what she was doing, she missed the warning signs of the birds' flight as an intruder disturbed them, so that her first intimation of his arrival was when the protective fronds of the willow were swept aside, and she looked up to see a very tall and very angry man standing glaring furiously at her.

'Robert.'

The curt demand for the child's attention gave away their relationship even before Robert started trembling against her, clinging on to her.

'It's all right, Robbie,' she whispered, soothing him, anger darkening her own eyes at Robert's father's lack of sensitivity.

'If you would kindly let go of my son . . .'

The words were a demand rather than a request, and immediately Sarah felt herself reacting against them, her already low opinion of him dropping several more notches as she reflected on his poor handling of the situation, and his apparent inability to see that his attitude was simply terrifying and upsetting his son.

'You must be Robert's father,' she commented, forcing back her anger and trying to stand up. Not an easy feat with Robert still clinging to her, but somehow or other she managed it, automatically assuming her classroom manner, forgetting how inappropriately it went with her casual clothes and almost childish pony-tail and make-up-less face, until she saw how at first angrily and even contemptuously she was being observed.

'Yes, I am,' he agreed flatly. 'But I've no idea who you are, or what you're doing with my son. However, I'll have you know that the police take a pretty dim view of child abduction.'

Abduction . . . Sarah sucked in a mouthful of air, too stunned by what he was implying to be able to respond verbally.

Robert was clinging even harder to her now, and she wasn't sure which of them was shaking the most, Robert from fear or she from anger.

As she swallowed the air she had gulped she retaliated with some heat.

'Yes, and they take an equally dim view of . . . of parental cruelty.'

'Parental cruelty?'

He had started to walk towards them, and now he came to an abrupt halt. His skin was tanned but suddenly his face had lost all its colour. Not from shame or guilt, but from rage. She could see it glittering in his eyes. He had very, very pale blue eyes, like shards of ice, she had thought at first, but now suddenly they were burning so hot that she could almost feel the searing lick of that heat against her skin.

Unlike Robert, he wasn't fair-haired but much darker, although she noticed that his thick dark hair was touched faintly with gold at the ends as though he had at some time or other spent a long, long time in a very hot climate.

Surprisingly, though, facially he was very like his son, or, rather, Robert was a miniature version of him. They had the same bone-structure, the same nose, the same mouth, but whereas in Robert that full bottom lip trembled with baby emotion and vulnerability, in his father it betokened a sensuality and sexuality which made Sarah itch to distance herself physically from him, her body alive to a sense of danger that went far deeper than any immediate and conscious awareness of his anger and irritation. She didn't allow herself to ponder on this, though; she was far too concerned about Robert and his panic-stricken reaction to his father's arrival on the scene to have the time to concentrate on her own atavistic awareness of his father as a man...no, not as a man...as a male...a hunting, arrogant, sexual male being to whom she was a natural form of prey.

'Parental cruelty,' he repeated grimly now, jerking her attention back in focus. 'What the hell are you trying to say? What has Robert been telling you?' he demanded.

Without making any move towards her, without either raising his voice or using any kind of aggressive force, he was nevertheless attempting to intimidate her, and she responded immediately to that attempted intimidation, raising herself to her full height, her chin firming, her eyes steely and cool as they held his gaze.

'Robert hasn't said anything,' she told him not quite truthfully. 'He was in far too distressed a state. He's a very unhappy little boy,' she added pointedly, adding, to reinforce the point, 'He was on his way to Ludlow...to London.'

She saw the way the blood surged up under the other's skin, and knew how much he hated being confronted with the truth. In other circumstances she might have felt sorry for him. He was wearing an expensive business suit, and she noticed that his hands were badly scratched, and his shoes covered in dust, as though he had pushed his way relentlessly down the narrow stream-side path, desperately seeking his missing son. But motivated by what? Anger? She could certainly see that in his face, along with impatience and irritation, but what she could not see there was any love, any remorse, any guilt.

'Come here, Robert,' he was demanding tersely now, frowning when his son refused to obey him. He was plainly unused to dealing with children, Sarah suspected, and, thinking of the child clinging piteously to her side, she said quietly,

'Perhaps if I came back with you...?'

Immediately the tanned male face tightened in rejection, the blue eyes cold and biting as they studied her. She could see the refusal forming on his lips, but before he could speak Robert burst out frantically, 'I won't go back. I won't go with you...I hate you...I hate you...and Mummy hated you too.'

He was crying again, tearing, racking sobs that, if they weren't checked, could easily carry him into hysteria. Instinctively Sarah bent down and picked him up, lifting him in her arms, so that his face was buried in the hollow of her throat, his small arms wrapping fiercely round her as she rocked and soothed him.

As she talked quietly to him she heard his father cursing under his breath.

He shot back a cuff and glanced at his watch, and the sympathy she had started to feel for him fled as Sarah heard him say edgily, 'That's enough, Robert. Look, I've got a meeting in half an hour...'

He must have seen the contempt, the dislike that flashed through her eyes, Sarah recognised, because he stopped speaking, his mouth firming into a hard angry line before he told her acidly, 'I'm a businessman as well as a father. I have a responsibility to my workforce as well as to my son. The outcome of an important new contract is in the balance here, and this meeting is a crucial one. Without it...well, let's just say that without it I could have to let some of the workforce go. Why on earth he had to choose today of all days to play up like this... You do realise that Mrs Jacobs is out of her mind with worry, don't you?' he demanded of his son. 'She had to ring me at work to tell me you'd gone missing, and if it hadn't been for the fact that Ben saw you heading for the stream path... And as for you...' he gave Sarah an angry, bitter look ' ... surely you realise that a child of his age, on his own, has to have left home without those responsible for him knowing where he is, and instead of encouraging him you could at least have attempted to take him home.'

His accusation took Sarah's breath away, but before she could deny his statement he was speaking to his son again, reiterating curtly, 'We're going home, Robert.'

But, as Sarah had known would happen, Robert refused to let go of her, clinging desperately to her when his father tried to take hold of him.

It was, she knew, out of necessity and nothing else that the man was obliged to stand so close to her, close enough to put his arms around her as he tried to unwind Robert's hands from behind her neck. She could smell the hot man scent of his skin, see the tiny pores of his face, dark where his beard would grow, his lashes a thick and enviably long fan against his skin as he frowned over his impossible task.

Uncomfortably aware of just how she was reacting to him, of the tiny female ripple of unexpected and unwanted response that jarred through her body, Sarah tried to step back from him, driven, as much by her need to put some distance between them as by her desire to help his son, into saying huskily, 'Look, it would be much easier if I came back with you.'

She could see the refusal ... the rejection ... and his dislike in his eyes as they focused brilliantly on her. He was still far too close ... far, far too close, she realised as she felt her breath stop in her throat, and her heart started to pound unevenly.

'I'm not going back. I want to go and live with Mrs Richards,' Robert was protesting, still clinging to her, adding piteously, 'Don't let him take me. I hate him.'

'Oh, for God's sake! Very well, then, you'd better come back with us. It's this way.'

Some people had no sense of gratitude, Sarah reflected grimly as he turned on his heel, patently expecting her to follow, but to her surprise he

stopped, lifting back the branches of the tree so
that she could step through, and then picking up
her rucksack before saying more quietly to Robert,
'You've got two legs, Robert, and you're far too
heavy for...'

'Sarah. Sarah Myers,' Sarah supplied automatically for him.

'...for Miss Myers to carry you all the way back
to the house.'

'Don't want to walk,' was Robert's response, his
bottom lip jutting out stubbornly as he turned his
head and looked at his father. Sarah's neck was wet
from his tears and she felt a wave of tenderness and
concern wash over her as she willed his acerbic
parent to at least try to understand and to have some
compassion for him.

'Very well, then, if you won't walk I'll carry you.'

As she felt the way Robert shrank back from his
father Sarah's tender heart ached for the little boy.

'Why don't you show me the way, Robert?' she
suggested, gently putting him down but protec-
tively keeping her own body between him and his
father as she took hold of his hand.

As she turned her head she saw that her gesture
had not been lost on Robert's father. His mouth
was curved into a line of bitter cynicism.

'Quite the little mother, aren't you?' he goaded
her grimly. 'What is it about your sex that makes
you so obsessively unable to behave with any kind
of logic where children are concerned? Can't you
see that he's——?'

'That he's what, Mr...?' Sarah intervened furiously, challenging him.

He looked at her, frowning as though surprised by both her attack and her desire to know his name.

'Gray. Gray Philips,' he introduced himself flatly. 'And you must be able to see that Robert is deliberately working himself up into a hysterical state.'

Quietly, so that Robert couldn't overhear her, Sarah contradicted equally flatly, 'No...what I see is a little boy who's lost everyone who loves him...a little boy who has apparently been left in the charge of a woman who neither likes nor cares about him...a little boy who has no one he can turn to other than his dead mother's housekeeper.'

Sarah knew that she was being deliberately emotive, but she couldn't help it. There was something about this impatient, critical man that pushed her into needing to bring home to him his child's emotional plight. 'What I can also see is that *you* don't appear to know very much about children, Mr Philips.'

Sarah drew in her breath at the way he looked deliberately at her own bare left hand before taunting softly, 'And you do? Do you have children of your own, then?'

To her mortification, Sarah felt her skin flushing as she was forced to admit, 'No...no, I don't.'

'Then I suggest you wait until you do before you start handing out the homespun advice,' he told her grittily.

Thoroughly incensed by his attitude, Sarah corrected him impetuously, 'I might not have any children, but professionally——'

'Professionally?' Gray Philips cut in sharply, frowning at her. 'What exactly does that mean? What exactly *is* your profession?'

'I'm a teacher,' Sarah told him, wondering even as she said the words just how much longer they would be true, and then pushing her fears and doubts behind her as she felt Robert's hand trembling in her own.

No matter how much she might dislike his father, she was not helping Robert by allowing her antagonism to take hold of her.

He 'hated' his father, Robert had said with childish intensity, and Sarah had not missed the brief look of pain that had touched Gray Philips's mouth as he had listened to his son's rejection of him. Despite her sympathy with Robert, she had to acknowledge that his father had every right to insist on taking the little boy back home.

She could not stop him from doing that, but what she *could* do was to go with him and to satisfy herself as much as she could that it was the confusion and grief of losing those people that he loved that was upsetting Robert so much and not any actual mistreatment by his father.

Oddly, despite his antagonism towards her, she could not quite convince herself that Gray Philips was mistreating his child. He had been too angry for that... his reaction to his son's disappearance too free of guilt and deception to suggest that he knew exactly why Robert had been running away.

He was walking ahead of them now, pausing to hold aside the vicious brambles blocking the path, his frown deepening as he saw the way Robert clung to her side.

It was twenty minutes before they were in sight of the village, but Gray Philips didn't walk towards it, instead branching off on to an even narrower and more overgrown path, which came to an abrupt end outside a solid wooden gate set into a high brick wall.

Gray Philips opened the gate for her, standing to one side so that she and Robert could precede him through it. Out of good manners, or as a means of ensuring that...that what? That she didn't pick Robert up and run off with him... What chance would *she* have had of outpacing a tough adult male like him?

The garden inside the brick wall was overgrown, the brambles even thicker than those on the path outside. Beyond the wilderness of undergrowth a cordon of trees guarded a green lawn and formal flowerbeds, and beyond that lay the house, all mellow brick and unevenly leaded windows.

It was old, Sarah recognised, Elizabethan, and much, much larger than her cousin's farmhouse.

Whatever Robert's father might not be, he was quite obviously a very wealthy man. But wealth did not buy happiness, and, even while she was admiring the house, she was not envying him the money that had enabled him to buy it. What good was money when his son was so obviously afraid of him...when his wife had presumably left him? Had *she* been afraid of him as well? But she must have loved him once. She had married him, after all...they had had a child.

A tiny shudder went through her as she recognised the dangerous course of her thoughts. To question someone's personal life so intimately and intensely, even within the privacy of her own thoughts, was so alien a response within her that she instinctively recoiled from acknowledging what she was doing.

Robert's footsteps lagged as they crossed the lawn. He was holding back, dragging his feet. His father stopped, frowning down at both of them.

'Is Mrs Jacobs still here?'

Sarah found she was holding her breath, praying that Gray Philips would deal sensitively with his son... would hear as she did the thread of fear that ran beneath the words.

If he did, he gave no sign of it.

'No, she isn't,' he told Robert curtly, and then, as though unable to stop himself, he dropped down on one knee in front of the small boy and placed his hands on his shoulders, demanding gruffly, 'Robert, why did you do it? *Why* did you run away? You *must* have known how worried Mrs Jacobs would be. You know you aren't allowed to go outside the garden... you know.'

Robert was still clinging to Sarah's hands. He had started to tremble violently, and tears poured down his face as he burst out passionately, 'I don't like it here. I want to go home... I want Nana... I want Mrs Richards. I don't like it here.'

Immediately his father's hands dropped from Robert's shoulders. His face was in shadow as he turned slightly away, his voice harsh and low as he said roughly, 'Robert, your grandmother is dead. You *know* that.'

He stopped as Sarah made an instinctive sound of shocked distress.

'What do you want me to do?' he challenged her. 'Lie to him? Pretend that none of it happened . . . that his mother, her lover and his grandmother are still alive?

'Come on, Robert. Let's get you inside, and this time no running away.'

As he stood up he took hold of Robert's arm, firmly taking charge of him, but Robert still clung to Sarah, pleading with her not to leave him.

His father might not be actively unkind to him, but he seemed to have little or no idea of how to deal with him, Sarah recognised as she instinctively tried to soothe Robert's panic, smoothing the soft hair back off his hot face as she promised, 'If you're a good boy and go with your father now, Robert, I'll come and see you tomorrow if you like.'

'There's no need for that.'

She met the look Gray Philips gave her with an equally challenging one of her own.

'Not according to you,' she agreed coldly. 'But Robert——'

'I don't want you to leave me. I want you to stay with me,' Robert said, and burst out crying.

Kneeling down beside him, she tried to comfort him as best she could.

'I can't stay now, Robert,' she told him. 'My cousin will be wondering where I am, but I promise I'll come and see you tomorrow.'

She looked defiantly at Gray Philips as she said the words, challenging him to refuse to allow her to see his son, and then, before Gray could say anything to her, and desperately trying to blot out Robert's tearful pleas to her to stay, she turned her back on both of them and hurried back towards the wooden gate.

CHAPTER TWO

HALF an hour later, as she walked towards her cousin's house, Sarah was still trembling with a mixture of shock and disbelief. She still could not entirely believe it had all actually happened. That poor little boy. He had been so upset... and his father had been so remote... so... so irritated and impatient... so completely unaware of how to respond to his son's misery and despair.

Sally was in the garden when Sarah opened the gate, dead-heading her roses.

'Are you all right?' she asked with some concern. 'You look upset.'

Sally was frowning when Sarah had finished explaining to her what had happened.

'Gray Philips... I'd heard that his son had recently come to live with him. The boy's mother, Gray's ex-wife, was killed in a car accident. She was pretty wild, according to local gossip. She was having affairs with other men almost before the ink had dried on their marriage certificate.

'I never met her, but apparently they separated before the little boy was born. I believe that Gray fought for custody of him, but lost, and that there were difficulties over access, which might explain the child's apparent antipathy towards his father. It must be very traumatic for him.'

'Yes, dreadfully,' Sarah agreed vehemently. 'The poor little mite was in a terrible state.'

Sally's eyes rounded.

'I didn't mean for the boy, I meant for his father... Gray.'

When Sarah frowned she asked quietly, 'Think about it. You've never been allowed to see your child, never had anything to do with him, and suddenly he's there living with you... hating you... probably blaming you for his mother's death. Imagine the state he must have been in when he found out that Robert had gone missing.'

Sarah's frown deepened. Sally was making her feel quite guilty... as though *she* had somehow been unfair towards Gray Philips, as though she had *deliberately* misjudged and condemned him.

'So you're going back to see him, the little boy, tomorrow, then?' Sally asked her.

'I promised I would, although his father wasn't very pleased.'

Sally gave her a thoughtful look.

'You're such a soft touch,' she told her wryly, 'but don't get too involved, will you, love? Rumour has it that Gray Philips is a man who, because of the breakdown of his marriage, doesn't have a very good opinion of our sex.'

'That's his problem, not mine,' Sarah responded firmly, and yet she was aware of a sense of dismay as she listened to her cousin's words, even though they only confirmed what her instincts had already told her.

And yet why *should* she feel dismayed? Gray Philips meant nothing to her; she hadn't even particularly liked him, and she certainly hadn't liked the way he was treating his son.

But she *had* responded to him physically. She *had* been very, very intensely aware of him as a man, aware of him in a shockingly sexual and intimate way that was totally foreign to her nature.

She had had a brief love-affair when she was at university, a relationship with a fellow student which had lasted a little over six months, but the sexual side of that relationship had never been as important to her as the emotional one. Even before she was ready to admit that she had fallen out of love with Andy, she had lost all interest in him sexually.

Since then she had been too busy, her life filled with too many other things to allow her the time to develop a committed relationship. She had male friends, went out on dates, but none of the men she knew had ever had one tenth, one hundredth of the effect on her that Gray Philips had had.

Trembling a little, she pushed that knowledge away from her, not wanting to confront or analyse it.

Beside her Sally was saying, 'I don't know about you, but I'm starving. Let's go in and have something to eat.'

Over dinner that evening Sally related the events of Sarah's encounter to Ross.

'Gray Philips...' his eyebrows rose '...hmm. That's interesting. What did you make of him, Sarah? He's very well thought of by the local business community. A sort of local boy made good. He took over an ailing family business when his uncle died, a light engineering concern in Ludlow, and he's managed to turn it right round and make it very successful. I have met him, although I don't know him very well. He's the sort who seems to prefer to keep himself to himself. Doesn't play golf... and he isn't a member of the new private sports centre that's opened outside Ludlow recently, and yet he certainly looks pretty fit.

'I had heard that he'd got his son living with him. My boss happened to mention the other day that Philips had been in touch with him, asking if his wife could recommend a good agency to supply him with someone to take charge of the child. Apparently he's been having problems in that direction. A wealthy single man...' Ross gave a small shrug. 'It seems the kind of woman he wanted to employ is reluctant to work in a household without another woman in it, and the kind that *does* want the job seems to be more interested in keeping him company than his son. He has got a housekeeper now, though, I believe.'

'Elsie Jacobs from the village,' Sally told him, pulling a face. 'And you know what *she's* like. Hardly the ideal person to have charge of a small child.'

'Mm. So what did you think of him, then, Sarah? Impressive, isn't he?'

'If you happen to like arrogant, bad-tempered and completely insensitive men, then I suppose he is,' Sarah agreed tartly.

Ross loved to tease her, and was constantly telling her that it was time she found herself a man and settled down, so she knew quite well what lay behind his question. This time, though, she wasn't going to rise for Ross's very obvious bait, nor his assumed mock-chauvinistic pose.

'It's the little boy, Robert, I feel sorry for,' Sally told her husband. 'From what Sarah was saying, he was almost distraught. He was trying to run away to London to find his grandmother's housekeeper. It must have been awful for him to lose everyone he loved, everyone who was familiar to him, like that.'

'Mm... although by all accounts his mother was far from the madonna type,' Ross interrupted. 'People locally don't seem to have a very high opinion of her, but then, I suppose, with Gray being local and her not, and the marriage only lasting for such a short time... And to deny Gray any kind of access to the boy...'

'Surely no court would do that without good reason?' Sarah pointed out, frowning.

'Well, you'd think not, but get yourself a good enough lawyer and who knows? And apparently she, the mother, was pretty good at putting on a performance when she deemed it necessary, whereas Gray, from what I know and have heard of him, isn't the type to actively sue for people's sympathy and compassion.'

'No, he isn't,' Sarah agreed feelingly, remembering how much Robert's father had antagonised *her* with his curt dismissal of her and his manner towards his son.

Ross shot her a very thoughtful look.

'All the same, he's very well thought of locally, and he's done quite a lot for the community.'

'Pity he hasn't done something for his son,' Sarah said grimly. 'If you could have seen him ... He was so upset ... so ... so unhappy.'

Ross frowned. 'You're not trying to suggest that Philips is actually harming the boy in some way, are you?'

Immediately Sarah shook her head.

'No ... at least not in any physical sense, and not deliberately, but emotionally... There doesn't seem to be any kind of bond between them at all. I suspect he ... Gray Philips looks on his son as just another responsibility, a burden he's had to assume. He seemed more concerned about a meeting he was supposed to attend than Robert ... and, of course, to Robert he's a stranger. If there hasn't been any contact between them since Robert's birth ...'

'And if, as you seemed to think was the case, his mother talked to him about Gray as though he was some kind of monster, he's bound to be afraid, isn't he?' Sally put in.

'Not an easy situation for any man to deal with, but in Gray Philips's present position it must be doubly difficult,' Ross commented, explaining, 'There's been some talk of a large multi-national wanting to take over the company. Gray is the major shareholder, but there are other family members holding shares, who, it seems, are in favour of the take-over because it will give them instant cash. Gray, on the other hand, quite naturally wants to retain ownership of the business, so there's an awful lot of behind-the-scenes negotiating going on. I suspect that ultimately he'll have to buy out the other shareholders; that will mean raising one hell

of a lot of money. No, I shouldn't want to be in
his shoes right now,' Ross concluded.

That night in bed, for the first time since her his-
toric and depressing interview with her superiors,
Sarah found that it wasn't their criticisms of her
that were going round and round in her brain as
she tried to go to sleep, but that instead she was
reliving her run-in with Gray Philips.

Strange how powerful the human mind was.
Without even the slightest conscious effort of will
she could mentally visualise him in such clear and
sharp detail that she could see the changing expressions cross his face; could hear the strong male
sound of his voice; could picture each gesture, each
movement he had made, almost as though the man
himself were there with her.

She turned over in bed, fiercely closing her eyes,
trying to block him out of her mind. It didn't matter
what Ross had said to her; she still felt that Gray
Philips could have done more, ought to have done
more to help his son. That poor little boy, to be so
cruelly robbed of those he loved ... to be removed
from a familiar and loved environment to one that
to him must appear totally hostile and unfriendly.
To be forced to live with a father who all his young
life he had been told was someone who did not love
him.

'I hate you,' Robert had said to his father with
all the vehemence of a frightened child, and just
for a moment Sarah had thought she had seen some
flicker of emotion burn in those so cold ice-blue
eyes. But what that emotion might have been she
did not know. Anger and impatience most

probably...certainly he had not displayed any other kind of emotion...any kind of warmth or love.

Perhaps in one way it *had* been wrong of her to promise to visit Robert without first obtaining his father's permission...perhaps she had done so deliberately because she had known that that permission would have been withheld, but how could she have lived with herself if she had deliberately and uncaringly turned her back on the little boy, shrugging her shoulders and telling herself that he was not her concern? No, she could not have done that. It ran completely counter to her whole nature. Tiredly she allowed herself to drift towards sleep.

'Look, why don't you take my car? I shan't be using it today, so you might as well.'

They were sitting having coffee in the kitchen, and Sally's offer of the use of her car made Sarah say gratefully, 'Well, if you're sure you don't mind, although I'm not sure how to find the house. The path went to a back gate and...'

'I've got a map of the village. The house isn't difficult to find. I'll get the map and show you...

'It was Gray Philips's grandfather who originally bought it,' Sally explained when she returned with the map, which she spread out on the kitchen table, pinning it down with her half-full mug of coffee.

'Gray's father was the older brother and should have inherited both it and the business, but he was in the army. He was killed in action when Gray was quite small. At least, that's what Mrs Richards told me. His mother apparently remarried and went to live in America, leaving Gray here. He was brought up by his grandfather, his uncle never married, and—again according to Mrs Richards—Gray was sent to boarding-school and then on to university, so that he virtually only spent his holidays here when he was growing up.'

Sarah was frowning as she listened to her cousin. Against her will she felt an aching tenderness, an awareness of how very lonely Gray Philips's childhood must have been, but surely that loneliness should have made him more compassionate towards his own child and not less? Then again, she knew enough about psychology to know that an adult would often inflict on his or her own children the same miseries they themselves had suffered, sometimes deliberately, but more often than not quite subconsciously, unaware that, out of their own deeply buried pain and resentment, they were unable to let go of the past and their subconscious resentment of another child, *their* child, enjoying a happier childhood than they had known.

Most people when confronted with such a truth were both appalled and angry, repudiating it immediately, even when it was explained to them that they were not consciously aware of what they were doing.

Was Gray Philips like that? Did he subconsciously resent his son's happiness?

She was leaping to unfounded conclusions, Sarah warned herself as she forced herself to concentrate on studying the map... allowing her emotions to take control of her. What Robert needed right now was not someone to reinforce his lack of trust and love for his father, but someone to gently encourage him to form a bond with Gray.

That task was not hers, she warned herself half
an hour later as she got into Sally's car. All *she*
could do was to try to comfort Robert as best she
could and to gently point out to him the dangers
of trying to run away. It was a pity that Gray Philips
had not taken the trouble to find someone more
sympathetic and understanding than Mrs Jacobs to
take charge of his son, since he plainly was not prepared to give Robert the emotional comfort and
support he needed himself.

She found the entrance to the house easily
enough. Automatic gates swung open as she drove
towards them, admitting her to the gravel-covered
drive.

The front view of the house betrayed that it was
even larger than she had first imagined and built
in the traditional Elizabethan E-shape. The drive
swept round not to the front of the house, but
through a brick archway and into what had once
been the stable-yard. Parking her car here, Sarah
climbed out.

Was it her imagination or did the sound of her
shoes crunching over the gravel seem preternatu-
rally loud?

She walked round to the front of the house,
pausing to admire the double row of clipped yews
that framed the main path as she did so. Beyond
them in the distance she could see the shape of a
formal pond and the spray of a fountain. Reflecting that it must cost a fortune to keep the house
and garden in order, she mounted the steps and
pulled the bell chain.

For a long time nothing happened, and she was
just about to wonder angrily if Gray Philips had

given Mrs Jacobs instructions not to admit her,
when the door suddenly opened to the extent of its
safety chain and a small, familiar voice asked uncertainly, 'Is that you, Sarah?'

'Robert... Where's Mrs Jacobs?' she asked the
little boy as he reached up to release the safety
chain.

'She's gone home,' Robert told her when the door
was open and Sarah went inside. 'She said she
wasn't paid to look after the likes of me and that
I was getting on her nerves,' he added woefully.

The hall was low-ceilinged and beamed, with a
polished wooden floor and an enormous cavern of
a fireplace. It was immaculately clean and yet
somehow unwelcoming.

The oak coffer against the wall cried out for a
pewter jug full of flowers, the floor for a richly
coloured rug, and stairs with barley-sugar twisted
and carved posts and heavily worn oak treads led
to the upper storeys of the house. A window set
halfway up them in their curve let in a mellow shaft
of sunlight, and, even while she admired the heavy
wrought-iron light fitting that hung from the
ceiling, Sarah was wondering why no one seemed
to have thought to fit the window-seat with a
comfortable squashy cushion, and thinking how
bleak the house looked despite its shining cleanness.

'Are you here all on your own?' she asked Robert
as he took hold of her hand and started to tug her
in the direction of one of the doors leading off the
hallway.

'Yes. My father's gone to work.'

'And Mrs Jacobs has left. Is she coming back?'

'No.' Robert shook his head. 'She said she wasn't going to set foot in this place again. At least not while I was here. Children are a nuisance, she said, and there are plenty of places she can work where she doesn't have to put up with them.' Tears suddenly brimmed in his eyes as he turned to look at her. 'My father is going to be cross with me, isn't he? But it wasn't my fault that I spilt the milk. I slipped on the kitchen floor.'

Sarah felt a mingling of anger and disgust. How could any father leave his child in the sole charge of a woman as plainly unsuitable as Mrs Jacobs, and how could any woman walk out on a six-year-old child when she knew there was no one to take charge of him, and when she must also know how vulnerable he was?

Robert pushed open a door which Sarah saw led into the kitchen. Her frown deepened when she saw the pool of milk marking the stone floor, its surface ominously broken by shards of glass. Had Mrs Jacobs really left without cleaning up the broken glass? It seemed that she had.

Quietly telling Robert not to go near the broken glass, Sarah set about cleaning up the mess.

While she was doing so he started to explain tearfully to her how the milk had been spilt when he was pouring it into his breakfast bowl of cereal.

The fridge from which he had taken the milk had a freezer section beneath it, and a handle surely far too high for the easy reach of a child of six.

When she heard how he had dragged a stool across the floor and climbed up on it to open the door, apparently while Mrs Jacobs was sitting down drinking a cup of tea, she was so angry both with

Mrs Jacobs and with Robert's father that she felt it was just as well that neither of them was there for her to vent her anger on them.

Surely the older woman must have realised the potential danger of a child of Robert's age climbing on a stool to open a fridge door? And surely in any case the little boy should not have been left to get his own breakfast?

Not wanting to pry and take advantage of his innocence, Sarah nevertheless had to ask him why Mrs Jacobs had not poured out the milk for him.

'She said it wasn't her job to feed me,' he told Sarah. 'And, besides, she was very cross. She said I didn't deserve any breakfast after what I'd done yesterday. She said I ought to be whipped and locked in my room.' His face grew shadowed and fearful. 'You won't...you won't tell my father about the milk, will you, Sarah?'

'Not if you don't want me to,' Sarah assured him, mentally crossing her fingers. She had every intention of making sure that Gray Philips knew exactly what she thought of a man who left his child in the sole charge of a woman like Mrs Jacobs.

It was almost lunchtime, and when she discovered that because of the accident Robert had not had any breakfast she opened the fridge and stared in disgust at its meagre contents. The freezer section below it was packed with microwave dishes and TV dinners, but there was nothing, as far as she could see, nutritious enough for a growing child...no fresh fruit, no fresh vegetables, nothing in the fridge that could in any way constitute the ingredients for a well-balanced healthy meal.

The bread-bin, when she found it, held half a loaf of dry, unappetising white bread, although the biscuit barrel was well stocked. Sarah turned away from this in disgust to announce firmly, 'Robert, you and I are going to do some shopping.'

It was warm enough for Robert to go out in his shirt and shorts, but before they left Sarah found an envelope in her handbag and wrote down a brief note on it, leaving it propped up on the kitchen table in the unlikely event of Mrs Jacobs's alerting Gray Philips to the fact that she had left Robert on his own and his coming home to ensure that he was safe.

Since she had no keys to any of the doors, she had to leave the back door unlocked, and as they drove away she prayed that no one would break into the house while she was gone.

In their nearest market town they had a good selection of food stores, so there was no need for her to drive as far as Ludlow.

After they had parked the car and collected their trolley she asked Robert what he liked to eat, and was pleased to discover from his answers to her questions that his mother had obviously been very strict about a healthy diet.

However, when she made some comment about his mother, he shook his head and told her, to her surprise, 'But I didn't live with Mummy and Tom. I lived with Nana. There wasn't room for me at Mummy's house, and besides...' He scowled and dragged his toe along the floor, telling her gruffly, 'Tom didn't like me. Peter's father liked him,' he added wistfully, causing Sarah to cease her inspection of the shelves and pause to look at him, asking questioningly,

'Peter?'

'He was my friend at school,' Robert told her. 'He lived with his mummy and his daddy. His daddy used to play with him. He was teaching Peter to play football,' he told her enviously.

Poor little scrap. Sarah ached to pick him up and hug him and to tell him that it wasn't his fault, that he had just been unlucky in the adult males in his life, because she could see the fear in his eyes, the belief that it was somehow his fault that first his mother's lover and then his own father had rejected him.

It seemed odd, though, that, after going to all the trouble of obtaining sole custody of him and refusing to allow his father to see him, his mother should then allow him to live full-time with his grandmother.

She was frowning a little over this as she scanned the shelves. She had plenty of cash with her, money she had brought with her when she had arrived from the city and which so far she had had no need to spend, thanks to the generosity of her cousin. According to Sally and Ross, Gray Philips was a wealthy man, and certainly wealthy enough to provide his son with a proper diet, so there was no need for her to scrimp on her purchases.

She could only marvel at the quality and training of a housekeeper who apparently was content to feed a grown man and a growing child on precooked frozen microwave meals. There was nothing wrong with such things for emergencies or days when cooking was inconvenient or impossible, but as a sole source of food...

As she paused to ask Robert if he liked fish she tried not to contemplate how Gray Philips was likely to view her interference.

Her shopping complete, she and Robert headed back to the car. He was chattering to her about his grandmother as they did so, and Sarah could tell how much he missed her—more, it seemed, than he missed his mother, but then, if he had lived with his grandmother... It would account for that oddly old-fashioned air he had about him at times, that grave, almost too adult manner that set him apart from the other children of his age that she knew.

Once they were back at the house she was re- lieved to find that there had been no intruders, but neither, it seemed, had Mrs Jacobs changed her mind and returned.

Had the woman no sense of responsibility, to leave a six-year-old child completely on his own?

After she had made Robert some lunch and seen him clean his plate she asked him if he knew what time his father normally came home from work. One thing was certain: there was no way she could leave Robert here on his own, which meant that she would have to wait with him until Gray Philips returned.

Robert shrugged his shoulders in response to her question. His father, it seemed, came home at a variety of different times, and she was appalled to discover from his artless chatter that more often than not the boy had been left by the housekeeper to get his own supper and get himself ready for bed, Mrs Jacobs having apparently threatened him that he would be in serious trouble if his father came home and found him still up.

The housekeeper seemed to have reinforced Robert's fear of his father by using Gray as a threat against him, but, angry as she was with the other woman, Sarah was even more angered by Gray Philips himself. Surely anyone with an ounce of sense must have known what was going on ... must have seen what was happening? Which meant either that Gray Philips couldn't be bothered with his son, or, even worse, simply didn't care.

Once she and Robert had washed up from lunch she telephoned Sally and explained the situation, adding that she felt she had to stay with Robert until his father returned.

'Yes, of course you must,' Sally agreed firmly, denying that it would cause her any problems if Sarah kept her car. When Sarah explained to her what she had found when she had arrived at the house, Sally told her, 'Well, I'm not entirely surprised. Mrs Richards was here this morning, and she was saying that Mrs Jacobs is the last woman fit to have charge of a small child. Apparently she detests children.'

After she had replaced the telephone receiver Sarah reflected that Gray Philips, as a local, must surely know of his housekeeper's reputation, and yet he had still left her in charge of his son.

Unwilling to stray too far from the house in case Gray Philips returned, Sarah spent the afternoon in the garden with Robert. He was an intelligent child, if perhaps a little over-sensitive and in need of a slightly more robust attitude towards life. That was probably because he had had no adult male in

his life to pattern himself on, Sarah reflected as
Robert chattered openly about his life before he'd
come to live with his father, and confirmed that he
had been living with his grandmother and not his
mother and that, moreover, it did not seem as
though he had actually seen a great deal of his
mother.

At six o'clock they went inside, and at her
suggestion Robert went upstairs for a bath before
she made his supper. He insisted on her going with
him, and a little reluctantly she did so. She didn't
want Gray Philips to come back and think she was
prying round the house.

For that reason she had kept strictly to the
kitchen, firmly suppressing any temptation to open
the doors into any of the other rooms.

But now, with Robert pleading with her and in-
sisting that he would not have a bath unless she
came with him, she reluctantly followed him upstairs on to the wide-galleried landing with its polished board floor and its dark portraits.

Against one cream wall was another oak chest,
just as bare of any touch of homely warmth as the
one downstairs, and, remembering the profusion
of flowers she had seen in the garden, she itched
to be able to gather up some of them so that their
rich colours broke up the sombreness of the house.

Two passages led off the landing. Robert grasped
her hand and took her down one of them, stopping
outside the door at the end of the passage and then
opening it.

His bedroom was large, and surprisingly
thoughtfully and well equipped for a boy of his age.
There was a large toy cupboard against one wall,

a desk and chair, a comfortable single bed with a duvet on it depicting Teenage Mutant Hero Turtles. Beyond the bedroom was a door which Robert told her led to his bathroom.

The bathroom was as well equipped as the bedroom, with a shower as well as a bath, but there was a dirty rim round the bath and a pile of damp towels on the floor.

'Mrs Jacobs said she wasn't cleaning in here 'cos I was a bad boy,' Robert told her when he saw Sarah looking at the towels. His face clouded suddenly as he added almost tearfully, 'At Nana's I had my special things in the bathroom, my frogs and my boat, but Mrs Jacobs threw them all away. She said they were only for babies.'

Sarah's heart ached for him as she was torn between her feelings for Robert and her fury at the other woman's unbelievable lack of compassion and understanding.

'Never mind. Perhaps we could make a paper boat for you to sail for tonight,' she suggested, adding, 'It won't sail very well, though.'

Instantly Robert's face lit up. 'Could we really do that?' he asked her, so obviously thrilled by her suggestion that she laughed.

'Yes, if we can find some paper,' she assured him.

Instantly his face fell.

'I haven't got any paper. Mrs Jacobs took it all away because she said it was making a mess. There's some in the study, though. We could go down and get it.'

Sarah hesitated. The last thing she wanted to do was to start rooting around in someone else's house, knowing how much she would hate another person

invading her own privacy, and yet she had promised
Robert, and if he knew where the paper was . . .

The study, as he called it, was more of a small
library, complete with library shelves and an impressive stock of leather-bound books.

A huge partner's desk dominated the floor space,
even if the computer terminal on it looked slightly
out of place.

Two large bay windows overlooked the gardens,
their leaded lights glinting in the evening sunshine.
The window-seats in the bays were covered in faded
damask, the fabric adding a comfortable homely
touch to an otherwise austere room.

The paper, it seemed, was kept in the bottom
drawer of the desk, but when Robert tried to open
it it was too heavy for him.

A little unwillingly Sarah got down on the floor
beside him to add her efforts to his.

'What the hell's going on in here?'

Sarah froze as she heard the angry male demand,
feeling Robert creep closer to her as his father's
anger reached out to engulf both of them.

Feeling like a thief caught in the act of stealing
something, Sarah turned round slowly, wishing she
was standing up and not kneeling down; not a good
position in which to defend herself, and certainly
not a good position from which to confront
someone . . . especially not a someone who was
standing over her, glaring furiously down at her,
and apparently putting the very worst kind of con-
struction there could be on what she was doing.

'We were looking for some paper so that we could
make a boat to sail in the bath.'

Robert's uncertain, nervous little voice broke the hard silence.

Both adults focused on him but with very different expressions. Sarah's was soft and tender, her hand going out instinctively to touch his cheek, to offer him some kind of comfort and reassurance, while his father's, if anything, became even more grim and irritable.

'You were what? Would you mind explaining to me what's going on here?' Gray Philips demanded, turning to Sarah. 'And where the hell is Mrs Jacobs? *She* was supposed to stay with Robert until I got back.'

At her side Sarah felt Robert start to tremble and knew immediately that he feared his father would blame him for the fact that the housekeeper had left.

Without allowing herself to dwell on Gray Philips's reaction to what she was doing, she touched Robert gently on the arm and said softly to him, 'Robbie, you go upstairs and get ready for bed while I talk to your father, will you?'

He was more than glad to obey her suggestion, scrambling to his feet and almost running through the door and up the stairs.

Once she was sure he was out of earshot Sarah got to her own feet. She had taken off her shoes when she had kneeled down on the floor and they were a couple of feet away from her. Wishing she had them on for the extra inches they gave her, she drew her body up firmly and tilted her chin, defiance and determination mingling in the look she gave the man watching her.

His silence was, if anything, even more intimidating than his original anger, but there was no reason for her to be intimidated by him. He, after all, was the one who was responsible for Robert...who had left him, a child of six years old, alone in the house without any form of adult supervision.

Reminding herself of this brought little comfort, but it did enable her to say defiantly, 'It seems that Mrs Jacobs has left...'

CHAPTER THREE

SARAH'S heart was pounding far too rapidly. There
was a long, long silence before Gray Philips made
any kind of response to her statement, but during
that time the mental messages that passed between
them were as fiery and volatile as a box of fire-
crackers, and even before he demanded savagely,
'What?' Sarah knew that he was blaming her for
the housekeeper's defection.

'She left before I got here,' she told him quickly,
and then, fearing that he would transfer blame to
Robert, added bitingly, 'I should have thought that
as Robert's father the very least you could have
done was to ensure that you left him in the charge
of someone caring and responsible and not a
woman who everyone knows can't stand children.'

She saw from his expression that her goad had
hit home. His eyes hardened and then glittered with
dislike, but before he could say anything Sarah
continued angrily, 'Do you realise that she wasn't
even feeding him properly? He hadn't had any
breakfast. There wasn't a scrap of food in the house
suitable for a child of his age, and——'

'You have been busy, haven't you?'

The softly venomous words silenced her, with all
that he wasn't saying. The look he gave her reduced
her to the very worst kind of prying Nosy Parker
and made her writhe with self-guilt and mortification. What was I supposed to do, she wanted to

challenge him, let Robert starve? But she had too
much pride to attempt to defend herself. The real
guilt was, after all, his and not hers, she assured
herself.

'If you were so concerned for Robert's welfare
surely the most sensible thing would have been to
ring me?'

The words dripped acid that corroded her
composure.

'Perhaps if I had known *where* to contact you I
might have done exactly that,' she told him shakily,
reaction beginning to set in.

'Robert knows my office number.'

She could feel herself flushing. She ought to have
thought of that ... ought to have. She gnawed dis-
tractedly on her bottom lip, wishing now, when it
was too late, that she had not acted so impetuously
and emotionally, reactions which this man could
never, ever understand.

Her primary desire had been for Robert ... for
his well-being, but now all she could manage in her
own self-defence was a weak and shaky, 'I thought
I was doing the right thing.'

How had it happened? she asked herself in angry
despair. How had their positions been reversed so
that *she* was the guilty party, and he her accuser?
Wasn't *he*, after all, the one at fault, while she ... she
had acted simply out of a desire to protect Robert?

All she could do in her own self-defence was to
throw at him what she knew to be the dangerous
challenge of announcing, 'Even if I had known your
number, Robert seems to be more ...'

She stopped abruptly, unable to bring herself to accuse him of allowing his child to be afraid of him, even while she felt it was the truth.

Too sensitive ... too painfully careful of the feelings of others, and, because of those faults, too vulnerable to make a good teacher; that was what her superiors had said, and now their criticisms were resounding in her ears, telling her that she had every justification for accusing Gray Philips of, at the very least, not seeing the effect his irascible hard-edged manner was having on his son. She acquitted him of deliberately fostering Robert's fear, but in her eyes not to be aware of the little boy's misery and unhappiness was almost as great a crime.

Now, as she faltered into an uncomfortable silence, it seemed that Gray Philips did not share her reluctance to use the words she had felt unable to utter, because he completed her sentence for her, saying grimly, 'Robert seems to be what? More afraid of me than reassured by my presence—is that what you were about to say?'

His mouth curled contemptuously as he added, 'Let me give you a piece of advice, Miss Myers. Once you've started to level a criticism at someone, don't back off halfway through it. By doing so you're suggesting that you lack any real belief in what you're saying.'

Immediately Sarah retaliated, too angry this time to care if she offended him.

'That's not true,' she told him fiercely. 'Robert *is* afraid of you. If he weren't ...'

She stopped again, and dulcetly he supplied for her, 'If he weren't he'd turn to me for comfort and reassurance and not you—is that what you were

about to say? Hasn't it occurred to you that, as a
child who has only been used to female company,
Robert might not be so much afraid of me but
might instead be finding it difficult knowing how
to react to me?'

Sarah knew that her flushed face gave her away,
and once again she mentally cursed her own
emotional reaction to the situation.

Feebly she countered, 'But Robert's mother
was . . . had——'

'A lover? Indeed. In fact, she had a succession
of them.' He saw her face and smiled cruelly at her.
'You look shocked. It's the truth, but then, of
course, we aren't supposed to speak the truth about
the newly dead, are we? We're supposed to focus
on their good points.' His face became bitter and
closed up. 'As far as I'm concerned, my ex-wife
didn't have any good points, and for your information Robert didn't live with his mother but with
his grandmother; my ex-wife, having hounded me
through the courts to ensure that I was denied access
to my son, to ensure that I could have no real place
in his life, then casually handed him over to the
care of his grandmother. You see, Angela didn't
love Robert; she wasn't capable of loving anyone
other than herself.' He broke off and, in an oddly
vulnerable and out of character gesture, ran his
hand through his hair, an almost baffled expression darkening his eyes as though he himself
was as startled by what he had said as she was.

He looked, Sarah realised in that odd moment
when she saw him not as an antagonist . . . not as
the father of a vulnerable, frightened child, but as
a man, very tired. It couldn't be easy for him, to

become solely responsible for a child who, despite
the fact that he had fathered him, was a complete
stranger to him . . . a child, moreover, who was
coming through the trauma of the death of all those
people closest to him.

But, even so, to have left Robert in the charge
of a woman like Mrs Jacobs . . . By all accounts,
Gray Philips was a wealthy man . . . wealthy enough
to provide his son with a properly trained nanny.

Almost as though he had read her mind, he told
her less acerbically, 'I have spent most of today interviewing prospective nannies for Robert, so far
without success.' His mouth hardened fractionally
and Sarah remembered what Ross had said about
the problems Gray was reputedly having in finding
someone suitable to take charge of his son. 'I shall
be spending most of tomorrow doing exactly the
same thing, hopefully with better results.'

Even though she knew it was none of her
business, Sarah could not prevent herself from
asking, 'Since whoever you employ is going to be
looking after Robert, wouldn't it be wise to allow
him to have some say in your eventual choice?'

'And have him pick some blonde bimbo look-
alike of his mother?' he demanded in disgust.

A small shock of sensation ran through her as
Sarah listened to him. Later, trying to analyse it,
she was uncomfortably aware of an emotion that
if not actually jealousy was a pretty close relation
to it, although why she should be jealous of
Robert's dead mother she had no idea whatsoever,
unless it was because, from his bitterly derisive
words, Gray Philips had drawn for her a picture of
a woman so very, very different from everything

that she was herself. Although his words had been outwardly derogatory and unflattering, woman-like, she had immediately stripped away that outer wrapping of criticism, and had guessed from Gray Philips's description that his ex-wife had more than likely been extremely pretty... extremely feminine, and probably very spoilt and wilful in the way that such women were, expecting and receiving male indulgence as their rightful due.

It did not matter that she could reassure herself that no man would ever condescend to her in that kind of way, that her looks would never encourage any man to treat her as a pretty, brainless doll and that she was grateful for it; some small, hitherto unknown part of her had instantly and shockingly lamented the difference between herself and the woman Gray Philips had so harshly described.

So far all the indications had been that his ex-wife was someone he had disliked and despised, and very strongly so, but then wouldn't a man of his intelligence, who had experienced what he had experienced in his marriage and subsequent divorce, almost force himself to feel the kind of emotions that he felt the world would expect him to feel towards his ex-wife when perhaps secretly in the depths of his heart he...?

He what? Still loved her? What if he did? Sarah asked herself stoutly. His feelings for his ex-wife had nothing to do with her, even though they might explain his attitude towards his son.

Warily she digested her thoughts, acknowledging that it disturbed her that she should have such strong feelings about a man who was virtually a

complete stranger to her...just as he, Gray himself,
disturbed her.

Unwillingly she forced herself to confront the
truth she had been dodging since her first meeting
with him. He was different from all the other men
she knew; more...more dangerously male;
somehow, more...more sensual. Even more uncomfortably she was forced to acknowledge how
very aware she was of him as a man, a totally new
experience for her. She had come across more
handsome men, had had her fair share of teenage
crushes on unattainable pop stars and the like, but
this was the first time she had experienced such an
intense rush of physical awareness of a member of
the male sex, and it disturbed and distressed her,
all the more so because his attitude both towards
her and towards Robert surely proclaimed the fact
that he was the very opposite of all that she had
always believed would appeal to her in a man. There
was no softness about him, no gentle, caring tenderness...no hint that he had absorbed all the
lessons that his sex were supposed to have absorbed
over the last decade and emerged from that learning
process as a caring, thoughtful human being,
brought to the humble realisation of how much his
sex had sinned against hers over the generations and
eager to make amends for those sins.

And yet...and yet...she could not in all honesty
accuse him of being aggressively, sensually
male...of using his powerful sensuality...or even
of being overly aware of it. Irritation, impatience,
anger...these were the emotions he had shown her,
and now, as she stood there in front of him, she
was uncomfortably aware of being an intruder in

his home, of acknowledging how little *she* would have relished returning home at the end of a tiring day to find that a stranger appeared to have invaded that home in her absence.

These feelings made her say quickly, 'I'd ... I'd better go. Now that you're back...'

She was making for the door as she spoke, suddenly very, very anxious to be free of his disturbing presence, even while she acknowledged that he was not the one responsible for the effect he was having on her and that the fault was hers, if she was so feeble-minded and vulnerable as to allow herself to become sexually responsive to a man who was so plainly oblivious to her as a woman.

'Without saying goodbye to Robert?'

The dry words made her stop and flush as she heard the cynicism behind them, and what made it worse was that it was true, that just for a moment she had been so wrapped up in her own emotions and fears that she had almost forgotten about his little boy.

Now she said defensively, 'No... of course not. I was just going to ask you if you minded if I went upstairs and said goodbye to him.'

The look he gave her, accompanied by raised eyebrows and a cynical twist of his mouth, deepened her embarrassment and guilt.

'Be my guest,' he told her sardonically, adding, 'I'm sure you don't need me to show you the way.'

She wanted to protest... to explain to him that she had not been taking advantage of his absence and Robert's innocence to violate the privacy of his home, but she knew that her protests would only be met by a sardonic wall of cynicism, and, be-

sides, why *should* she explain or apologise? She
knew the truth, even if she also knew that he would
refuse to accept it.

Shakily she headed for the door, stopping uncertainly, waiting for him to step to one side so that
she could go through. When he did so she discovered as she walked past him that she was holding
her breath, as though she was desperately afraid of
somehow inadvertently coming into physical
contact with him, as though by holding her breath
she could somehow make herself smaller, but as
she approached him he stepped even further back
from her, allowing her plenty of space in which to
move past him, and neither did he make any attempt to accompany her as she went upstairs.

Robert was still in the bathroom. He looked up
anxiously when she walked in, his expression
turning to relief when he saw her. She explained to
him that she was about to leave, steeling her heart
against the look he gave her when he pleaded with
her to stay.

As a compromise she waited until he had finished washing, and then helped him to get dried
and dressed in the clean pyjamas she found in a
drawer. She noticed as she took them out that they
were brand-new, with the labels still inside them.
As she removed them Robert told her innocently,
'Mum was going to buy me some new ones but she
couldn't afford it.'

Sarah frowned as she helped him into them. She
had gained the impression that Robert's mother and
grandmother were comfortably off financially. Had
she been wrong, or had Robert's mother simply
been the sort of woman who was too selfish, too

self-absorbed to realise that her growing son needed new clothes, who had perhaps offloaded whatever guilt this neglect had caused her by claiming that it was a lack of money and not a lack of concern that had been responsible for such neglect?

Only once she had tucked him up in bed, and ensured that he was comfortable, did Sarah feel able to leave.

As she went downstairs she glanced at her watch, realising guiltily just how long she had been with Robert.

In the hall all the doors were closed. A sign that Gray Philips expected her to leave without imposing her unwanted presence on him a second time? Very probably. After all, he had made it quite clear how he viewed her presence in his home.

She was just about to open the front door, when she heard him saying from behind her, 'Not bothering to say goodbye, Sarah?'

There was so much sarcasm in his voice, so much unexpected criticism and condemnation of her manner of leaving, almost as though she was in some way deliberately trying to sneak out without having the good manners to observe the normal civilities, that she immediately felt as guilty as she had done when he had walked in and found her apparently rifling through his desk drawer.

As she had done then, she flushed to the roots of her hair, even while she cursed the vulnerability of her tell-tale fair skin.

'I . . . I didn't want to disturb you,' she told him nervously.

'No, I'm sure you didn't.' He was looking at her, studying her, and for some reason her embar-

rassment changed to a suffocating, acute awareness
of him, just as though something had touched a
deeply rooted sensual chord within her, so that her
whole body seemed to vibrate in response to that
awareness of him.

Still looking at her, he said silkily, 'What a pity
you didn't think about that before, isn't it?'

And then he walked up to her, forcing her to step
back from him in order to keep some distance between them.

For one crazy, stupefyingly out-of-character
moment she actually thought he was going to touch
her, to take hold of her...to... She swallowed with
difficulty, her attention unwittingly focusing on his
mouth, her pulses racing as she wondered what it
would feel like against hers...what it would feel
like if he *did* take hold of her...if he *did* bend his
head...if he did... One thing was for sure: he would
be no tentative, uncertain lover...and he would not
be inexperienced either. He would...

She closed her eyes, trying to dismiss her wild
thoughts, and while they were closed she heard the
sharp snick of the front door catch being unlocked.

The realisation that he had not intended to touch
her at all, but had simply been opening the door
for her, performing the small simple courtesy of
any householder in seeing a guest, wanted or
otherwise, off his premises, sent a sharply painful
wave of mortification grating against her too-tender
nerve-endings.

As he started to open the door she tried to rush
through it, desperately anxious to get away, not so
much from him, but from her own idiotic response
to him, but unfortunately in her rush to escape she

misjudged the width of the opening and jarred
herself painfully against the door-jamb, causing her
to cry out with the shock of the impact.

Now he did touch her, not as a would-be lover,
but as an impatient, grim adult confronted with the
idiocy of an unknowing child, holding her firmly
within his grip as he opened the door a little wider,
while saying, 'I have heard that some women are
inclined to mentally distort their body shape, but
even a child of six couldn't have got through that
space.'

His criticism stung. Impetuously she lied, 'My
cousin will be wondering what on earth has happened to me. I must get back.'

'Indeed, and those few vital seconds you could
have saved in squeezing through a barely open door
would have made all the difference. Strange, isn't
it, how you only became aware of the sudden rush
of time once you'd left Robert?'

There was nothing she could say, and now mercifully the door was open enough for her to walk
through it. All she had to do was to pull free of his
grip, which had mercifully relaxed, and try to
pretend to herself that her inelegant and hasty retreat was not making her look even more of an
idiot. As she fled towards her car she refused to
give in to the temptation of turning round to see if
Gray Philips was actually watching her as intently
as she felt him to be.

Of course, she would have to crash the gears of
her cousin's car, and send the gravel spinning as
she reversed the vehicle, and of course Gray Philips
would have to be watching her with an unreadable
expression on his shuttered face as she weakly gave

in to the temptation to look in the direction of the
front door before finally driving off.

Naturally, when she got back Sally wanted to hear
what had happened.

'You poor thing, you must have been embarrassed to death,' was her sympathetic comment
when Sarah explained how Gray Philips had walked
in and found her apparently going through his desk.
'Still, he must have been grateful to you for stepping
in like that and taking charge of his little boy.'

'Not so as you'd notice,' Sarah told her wryly.

'Poor chap. I don't envy him,' Ross remarked
later over a cup of coffee. 'It can't be easy for him,
having to take charge of the boy and to find
someone responsible to take care of him.'

Sally threw a cushion at him.

'Men—you're all the same, sticking up for one
another,' she accused him. 'What kind of father
would leave a six-year-old in the charge of someone
like Mrs Jacobs?'

'The kind who doesn't have any alternative,' Ross
told her drily.

'Umm . . . well, if you ever did that to our children——' Sally began, but he interrupted her,
getting up to carry the cushion back to her, telling
her provocatively, grinning at her,

'Well, I shan't have to, shall I . . . not with you
to look after them?'

Sarah tried not to feel envious of the rapport and
closeness between her cousin and her husband. Ross
might pretend on occasions to be the typical macho
male, but there was no doubt that their marriage
was very much one of equal partnership, and Sarah

had no doubt that when their children eventually came along both of them would take equal responsibility for them.

'Don't be too hard on Gray,' Ross said quietly to her now. 'It hasn't been easy for him. I happened to mention at work today that you'd got involved with his son, and one of the other men who was around when Gray was first married said that his wife was a first-class bitch. Rumour has it that she tricked Gray into marriage by allowing herself to get pregnant, and then, once she realised that, despite his money, he wasn't the type to go in for the kind of hectic social fast-lane life she wanted, she upped and left him, refusing to allow him any kind of access to the child. Apparently she even told him that if he tried to push for legal access she would tell the court that the baby wasn't his ... but she was quite happy to take the money he paid her... and all this from a man who openly admitted that when Gray first married her and brought her here he was bowled over by her looks. Looks which apparently were not matched by an equally attractive personality.'

'Well, that's as may be,' Sally interrupted her husband. 'But, if he was so keen to have access to his child, how come he's now so irritable and distant with him?'

Ross shrugged. 'Who knows? Perhaps he's afraid to let the boy get too close to him, or perhaps the boy won't let him. After all, from what I've heard, the mother wasn't the type to miss out on any opportunity to score off on Gray. Who knows what she might have told the boy? Can't be easy for Gray.'

'No. Well, let's hope he finds someone suitable
to take charge of him, and soon. Robert's already
tried to run away once, and a child of that age is
so dreadfully vulnerable. It makes me shudder to
think of what could have happened to him if Sarah
hadn't found him.'

'I didn't *find* him,' Sarah corrected her. 'He
found me, so to speak.' She was frowning as she
turned to Sally. 'Do you think he might try to do
that...to run away again?'

Only this afternoon she had gently tried to point
out to Robert the dangers of what he had attempted to do. His grandmother had, it seemed,
warned him of the dangers of speaking to strangers,
especially those with cars, but she had neglected to
explain why, and Sarah had been torn between
wanting to strengthen that warning with something
more concrete than his grandmother's vague
suggestion that strangers were dangerous and a reluctance to interfere in the upbringing of a child
who wasn't in any way connected with her.

'So shall we ask him or not?' she heard Sally
saying to her, and came out of her thoughts to discover that her cousin was apparently planning a
dinner party and that, moreover, she was asking
her if she thought she should invite Gray Philips.

'Don't ask me. I mean...'

'You're embarrassing her,' Ross told his wife, his
comment increasing Sarah's embarrassment rather
than alleviating it.

'Oh, Sarah, I'm sorry. I wasn't trying to
matchmake,' Sally told her immediately. 'No, it's
just that we haven't had a proper dinner party since
we moved in here, and now that this long com-

mission is almost completed I'm beginning to suffer
from a slight touch of cabin fever, although I
suppose officially the dinner party season doesn't
really start until the children go back to school. Still,
as I've always said, some rules are made to be
broken.'

'Why don't you admit that you're as curious as
hell about Gray Philips and that this is the only
way you can legitimately think of to satisfy that
curiosity?' Ross teased her.

Now it was Sally's turn to flush.

'Well, of course I'm curious,' she defended
herself. 'And Sarah isn't helping. My daily described him as "very much a man. You know what
I mean,"' Sally told them, imitating her cleaner's
manner, 'but you, Sarah...well, you haven't so
much as mentioned what he's like as a man...only
how you feel about his shortcomings as a father.'

She gave her cousin a distinctly speculative
glance.

'Is he as macho as Mrs Beattie seems to think?'

'I wouldn't describe him as macho exactly,' Sarah
told her truthfully, but even as she answered her
cousin's question she was acutely aware of all that
she was not saying...all that she was withholding,
even from herself...such as the way she reacted to
him physically...such as the way she had so stupidly, so cringingly willed herself into believing that
he'd been about to kiss her, even to the point where
she had almost actually experienced the sensation
of his mouth against hers.

'To be honest with you, I haven't really regis-
tered all that much about him,' she lied now. 'It's
his relationship with Robert that concerns me.'

'So you won't mind if I invite him to dinner, then?' Sally asked slyly.

What could she say?

'As long as I don't have to sit next to him. No, I don't mind at all,' she replied, striving to appear unconcerned.

But she had forgotten how well Sally knew her and all those small betraying mannerisms that gave away so much, although it was later on when the two of them were alone that Sally said quietly to her, 'Look, if it really does bother you, I won't invite Gray Philips round for dinner.'

'Bother me...of course it doesn't bother me...why should it?' Sarah retorted defensively, ignoring the look her cousin was giving her.

CHAPTER FOUR

Two days went by without Sarah either seeing or hearing anything of Robert or his father. She told herself that she was glad, that Gray Philips had obviously found someone responsible to take charge of his son and that the little boy was settling down in his new environment.

Sally, who had reluctantly gone back to work to finish her commission, was still making plans for her proposed dinner party, which had grown from the original intimacy of six or eight people to a number closer to twenty.

'Perhaps we ought to have a buffet party instead,' she murmured more to herself than to Sarah as they sat drinking their coffee one morning. 'Yes, a Sunday lunch buffet party. What do you think?'

'I think it sounds a lot of hard work,' Sarah told her honestly.

'Mm...maybe, but a buffet do would be much less work than a full-scale dinner party, and much more in line with my cooking skills,' Sally admitted with a grin, adding, 'Remember that dinner party I gave when I was going out with John Howarth?'

'Wasn't he the one who was the embryo chef?' Sarah asked her, her forehead crinkling as she tried to remember which of Sally's many boyfriends she was referring to.

'That's the one,' Sally agreed. 'I remember I was planning to serve a soufflé for pud, only something went wrong and I ended up giving them ice-cream and apple pie...do you remember?'

'Yes, I do, since I was the one who had to go hurtling out to buy the damn thing,' Sarah agreed feelingly.

'I never saw John again after that. I wonder why.' Both of them burst out laughing.

'Ah, well, back to work,' Sally explained, finishing her coffee. 'What are you going to do?'

'Take myself off for a long walk,' Sarah told her.

Sally frowned. 'You mustn't let this school business get you down,' she told her gently. 'I know you, Sarah. You're a delicate plant, all too easily inclined to withdraw and curl up inside yourself when you feel you're under attack. I wish I could do more to help you through this difficult time.'

'You *are* helping me,' Sarah assured her. 'But it's something I've got to sort out for myself. Who knows? Perhaps they're right and I'm not cut out for teaching.'

'But you love it so much, and besides...'

'What else can I do?' Sarah asked her drily. 'I don't know, but there must be something; after all, according to the Press, teachers are leaving the profession in droves, and they must be going somewhere.'

'Well, with your qualifications I'm sure you wouldn't have any problems in finding something else, although it would mean starting again, probably at the lower end of the career ladder.'

'Stop worrying about me,' Sarah told her cousin affectionately, smiling at her, but in reality she felt far from smiling as she reviewed the problems that lay ahead of her.

Did she really want to go back to teaching, to her old school, knowing her every move was being monitored and criticised? It was true that she loved teaching... loved her pupils, but wasn't it also true that she was over-inclined to become too emotionally involved with them? That was a flaw in her own personality and not something that could ever be entirely eradicated, no matter how much she might try to train herself to do otherwise. And yet if she wanted to continue with her career she was going to have to find a way of stopping herself from caring so deeply.

She walked for a long time, trying to resolve the feelings of guilt and inadequacy which had hung over her like a dark cloud ever since that fateful interview. It didn't matter how often she told herself that she was not a failure, she could not reassure herself; she had been tried and found wanting, and, no matter how much her friends and family tried to comfort her, they could not alleviate the burden of despair that knowledge had brought her.

And yet, if she left teaching, what was she to do? Retrain in another field? Which field, though?

It was late afternoon when she returned to the cottage, approaching it from the back across the fields, using the gate in the hedge at the bottom of the long garden rather than walking round to the front.

As she walked up the garden path Sally opened the back door, beckoning to her, and pressing her finger to her lips as Sarah frowned and called out, 'What is it? Is something wrong?'

'You've got a visitor,' Sally told her almost con-spiratorially. 'Gray Philips. I've put him in the

sitting-room. He's been here ages. I thought you'd
be back much earlier.'

Gray Philips! Why did he want to see *her*? Her
heart had started pounding erratically, and she was
conscious of a sense of anxiety coupled with a reluctance to see him. Her hair was all tousled from
her long walk, and she suspected that she must be
the complete antithesis of the women he was used
to... the women he admired and desired. She only
had to remember the way he had described his late
wife... the emotion she had sensed beneath the
cynical words he had used.

Stop that, she derided herself as she pulled off
her boots in the laundry-room, ignoring Sally's
desire for her to hurry.

'If he's waited this long, he can wait a little
longer. At least until I've combed my hair and
washed my hands,' Sarah told her grimly, unwilling
to admit even to someone as close as her cousin
how reluctant she was to see him.

'He's getting pretty impatient,' Sally warned her.
'I'll go and tell him you're here.'

Despite her intention not to hurry, once she was
upstairs in her room Sarah discovered that her
hands trembled as she washed them and that she
was combing her hair far faster than normal, while
anxiously scanning her unmade-up face and wishing
that it looked different... less ordinary. She even
told herself that the lipstick she was so unsteadily
applying was simply a confidence booster and
nothing more, but when she realised that she was
halfway through stripping off her old jeans and
shirt and exchanging them for a clean top and a

skirt she knew it was pointless trying to deceive herself any longer.

She stared down at the floor, shivering a little. What was the matter with her? Did she really think she was going to make an impression on Gray Philips as a woman simply because she was changing her clothes? Did she really not have the intelligence to know that, while initially clothes— or at least the right kind of clothes—might attract a man's visual attention, attraction, real, gut-wrenching physical awareness of the kind she had experienced for him had nothing to do with clothes, and everything to do with something far more subtle and sensitive?

She was simply not Gray Philips's kind of woman, and if she had any sense she ought to be thankful for that fact. Ross had suggested that his marriage had left him feeling bitter and antagonistic towards the female sex, and she suspected that, though he might be willing to enter a physical relationship with a woman, he would be extremely guarded where his emotions were concerned, while she...

Shaking her head, she pulled on her clean clothes. She had to stop this. It was not only dangerous; it was addictive as well. Instead of allowing her thoughts to stumble heedlessly down such forbidden paths she ought to be concentrating her mind on trying to work out just why Gray Philips had come to see her. Was it because of Robert? Had something happened to the little boy? Had he perhaps run away again?

Her fingers shook as she zipped up her skirt, mentally praying that that wasn't the case. But no, it couldn't be. Gray Philips would hardly have wasted so much valuable time waiting for her to return if Robert was actually missing.

She went downstairs, heading for the sitting-room. The door opened and Sally came out just as she approached it. Sally grimaced wryly at her and whispered, 'Rather you than me. Sexy he might be, but he's not exactly communicative, is he?'

When Sarah walked into the sitting-room Gray Philips was standing with his back to her, looking out into the garden.

She had walked in very quietly, her feet not making any sound on the thick pile carpet, but nevertheless he must have either heard her or seen her reflection in the window, because he turned round immediately.

To her own intense annoyance, Sarah heard herself apologising breathlessly, 'I'm sorry you've had such a long wait. I was out walking.'

What on earth was she doing? Why on earth did she feel this need to placate him almost?

The frown with which he had greeted her lifted, an oddly thoughtful look lightening his eyes as though he too was aware of the contradiction of her behaviour.

'I should have rung first,' he responded curtly. 'But, once I'd got here, it seemed foolish not to wait...although...I've got an appointment at five, so I'll come straight to the point if I may.'

When Sarah inclined her head he asked her coolly, 'Is it true, as I've heard on the local grapevine, that you're here to think about your future career and that although you're a qualified teacher you may not be returning to that career?'

His words were carefully chosen, Sarah recognised, so as not to antagonise her, and that in itself was surprising enough to make her focus on him.

He was watching her very closely, and had also closed the distance between them, so that there was only the length of the sofa between them.

A tiny pulse started beating frantically in her throat as all her fears and vulnerabilities came crowding in on her. She knew all too well what else he would have heard on that same grapevine, and reflected how cynically contemptuous he must have been on hearing the gossip.

It was that awareness that made her lift her head and face him challengingly to say almost as cooly as he had spoken to her, 'If you mean have my superiors suggested to me that it might not be a good idea for me to return to teaching because of my getting too involved with my pupils, then yes.'

The look he gave her made her skin flush vividly, although for once there was neither contempt nor anger in his eyes. Instead he was looking at her with something that in someone else she might have described as humour and approval, and yet the thought of this man having a sense of humour and approving of her seemed so remote as to be impossible... a trick of her imagination.

'And you haven't lined up a fresh job for yourself as yet?' he was asking her.

Sarah shrugged. 'No... not as yet.'

Her tone implied that it was not a line of conversation she wished to pursue and that neither were her future plans any of his business.

'Good.'

Good? What did that mean? Her eyes rounded as she looked questioningly at him. 'What does that mean?' she demanded bitterly, her introspective thoughts of the afternoon colouring her reaction to his satisfied exclamation. 'That you're glad I'm not inflicting either myself or my irrational emotions on a fellow employer?'

What on earth was she saying? she asked herself angrily as she fought to rein in her absurd over-reaction.

'What it means,' Gray Philips told her, ignoring her outburst, 'is that I'm glad you haven't committed yourself to a new job, because it means that I can ask you if you would contemplate coming to work for me.'

Going to work for him. Sarah felt her jaw drop as the shock of his words hit her.

'But I don't know anything about engineering,' she heard herself say stupidly.

There was a small pause, as though what she had said had taken him off guard, and then he was saying wryly, 'You won't need to. At least, not unless Robert suddenly develops an interest in it.'

'Robert? But——'

'What I'm asking you is whether you'd be prepared to come and work for me as Robert's companion and mentor,' he told her, forestalling her questions.

'You want me to look after Robert.'

Her shock showed in her voice and her face. After what had happened between them she had felt that she would be the last person he would want anywhere near his son. 'But I thought . . . you said . . . I thought you were interviewing nannies.'

'I was, but unfortunately none of them proved suitable—or, at least, four of them seemed to be well qualified for the job, but when I took your advice and introduced them to Robert he rejected them all. Then he told me that what he would really like was for you to look after him.'

Sarah was still staring at him. Whatever she had thought about him, however she had judged him, she had never, ever thought that he would allow his son—a son, moreover, whom he appeared to view more in the light of a nuisance than anything else—to sway his own judgement.

'But . . . you don't like me.'

She bit down hard on her bottom lip, wondering what on earth had happened to her common sense. What an idiotic thing, to say something that, no matter how true it might be, should never, ever have been voiced.

He seemed to think so as well, because his eyes darkened and his mouth thinned.

'I don't *have* to like you,' he told her grimly. 'Nor, for that matter, is it necessary for you to like me. I'm trying to put Robert's need first here, Sarah. Isn't that what you wanted me to do?'

The soft accusation was more of a taunt than an admission that he might have been wrong in his treatment of his son.

'But . . . but . . . I'm not trained for that kind of work,' she protested. 'I'm a teacher.'

'A teacher who, according to the local grapevine, is so soft-hearted that she spends more time trying to sort out her pupils' emotional problems than she

does in teaching them. A strong mothering instinct
isn't something that can be taught or learned,
Sarah.'

A strong mothering instinct. For some reason the
words brought a huge lump to her throat.

'But I'm not sure if I can make that kind of commitment,' she protested. 'And it wouldn't be fair
to Robert to allow him to become dependent on me
when——'

'I'm not asking you to make a permanent commitment to him,' Gray Philips interrupted her.
'That would be impossible and inadvisable, both
for him and for you, but I can't deny that at the
moment he's a very vulnerable little boy. For some
reason he seems to have developed a bond with you.
He is my son, Sarah, and quite naturally I want
him to be happy...to hopefully forget in time
that——'

'That's he's lost his mother and his grandmother?' Sarah asked him tautly. 'That would be
impossible and unfair. He needs to be *able* to remember them, to talk about them. And how can
he feel he can talk to you about them when you've
made it so clear how you view his mother?' She
broke off, aware that she had said far too much.

'I'm beginning to see why you're not suitable
teacher material,' Gray Philips told her unkindly.

She had to turn her head away so that he wouldn't
see the quick rush of tears to her eyes.

More out of hurt pride than anything else, she
heard herself telling him almost violently, 'I'm not
suitable as a substitute mother either, and if that's
what you want for Robert then I suggest you find
him one in a rather more conventional manner.'

'Remarry, you mean.' His eyes were as sharp and dangerous as splintered glass, his expression hard and bitter. 'Shall we abandon this emotional quagmire and get back to reality?' he demanded tersely. 'I'm not suggesting for one moment that you should provide Robert with substitute mothering. I'm merely trying to ascertain whether you would be interested in working for me as Robert's nanny. And if you *are* interested in doing so I must warn you that I shall want a written commitment from you to remain in my employ for a minimum of twelve months.'

Sarah wanted to refuse, to tell him that it was impossible for her to even contemplate working for him when it was plain that they could never get on. And it wasn't just that...there was also her dangerous awareness of him as a man.

'If you did take on the job I would be prepared to allow you a very free hand in your dealing with Robert.'

'Leaving you free to ignore him,' she accused bitingly.

The look he gave her only reinforced her doubts. Much as she liked Robert, much as she ached to be able to help the little boy, she could not work for his father.

'Don't give me your answer right now,' Gray Philips was telling her, ignoring her attempts to tell him that she had already made up her mind. 'I'll call round tomorrow and you can give me your decision then. No doubt you'll want to discuss my offer with your cousin and her husband.'

For some reason his tone irritated her. 'Why should I?' she demanded belligerently. 'I *am* an

adult and perfectly capable of making my own decisions about my life.'

'I'm sure you are, but most of us like to get the
views of those closest to us when we make major
changes in our lives.'

While she digested this silken comment Sarah reflected that she doubted that he had ever listened
to anyone else's views in his entire life. But he had
listened to Robert's, an inner voice reminded her.

He was already walking past her and heading
towards the door. In another minute it would be
too late for her to tell him that she had already
made up her mind and that she did not wish to
accept his offer of a job, and yet she was letting
him open the door, letting him walk away from her,
letting him assume that she was actually going to
consider his proposition when she knew, and surely
he must know too, that it simply could not work.

She was standing watching him drive away when
Sally came into the sitting-room and asked her
eagerly, 'Well?'

'Mm?' She turned round, unwilling to take her
eyes off the disappearing shape of his car. 'Oh . . . it
was nothing really. He wants me to look after
Robert for him, but he's stipulated that I would
have to commit myself to doing so for a period of
twelve months.'

'What? He's offered you a *job*?' Sally beamed
at her. 'Oh, that's wonderful. I was dreading your
leaving. It's been terrific having you here, especially with Ross having to work away so often.
Oh, Sarah, I'm so pleased.'

'I haven't accepted,' Sarah interrupted her. 'He's
coming back tomorrow for my reply, but——'

'But what? You'll take it, of course. I mean, what's twelve months? It will be a wonderful breathing-space for you...giving you time to think about what you really want to do.'

'I'm still employed as a teacher,' Sarah reminded her quickly. She was beginning to feel as though she was being sucked down into a quagmire...as though only she could see the impossibility of working for Gray Philips and the dangers it involved, but then, of course, Sally knew nothing about those disruptive, unwanted feelings he aroused within her, and she was certainly not going to tell her.

'Come on, love,' Sally coaxed her, 'you know as well as I do that you've been dreading the start of the new term. I know how good you are with children emotionally. How good you are at——'

'Mothering,' Sarah supplied sardonically for her.

Sally gave her a frowning look. 'You're too hard on yourself. Everyone knows how important a child's early years are, and everyone knows that in the majority of cases it's a child's mother who shares those years. You've said yourself how concerned you are for Robert, and here's your chance to help him.'

Sarah shook her head. 'I'm not so sure it would be a good thing,' she resisted stubbornly.

Sally gave her a shrewd look, and told her, 'Well, you've got twenty-four hours to think about it and, of course, the final decision must be yours.'

Which didn't stop her unsubtly pointing out all the advantages of accepting Gray Philips's offer throughout dinner and long after they had finished eating, and of course Ross fully supported her, adding his own approval and persuasion.

If it weren't for Gray Philips himself she would have been only too happy to accept the job, Sarah acknowledged as she lay in bed waiting for sleep to claim her. She liked Robert . . . felt drawn to him, and she knew she could help him. Was it really fair of her to put her own needs, her own vulnerabilities, before a child's? Surely she was capable of either dismissing or ignoring her awareness of his father? After all, she was pretty sure that Gray Philips would ensure that they had the minimum of contact with one another, and her role as Robert's nanny would mean that he was not likely to spend much time in the house while she was there to take charge of Robert. If she did take the job it would have to be on the condition that she did not live in, but commuted daily. Which meant that she would need a small car. Well, she had sufficient savings to allow her to buy one . . . but *why* was she thinking along such lines when she had already made up her mind that she simply was not going to take the job?

'There's a letter here for you,' Sally announced over breakfast as she went through the post. 'Mm . . . looks very official,' she commented as she handed it over.

A tiny thrill of nervous apprehension went through Sarah as she opened it, her breakfast ignored as she read it once and then a second time.

'Sarah, what is it? What's wrong?'

It took Sally's anxious question to lift Sarah's head from the letter, her eyes vague and dark with shock as she said unsteadily, 'They're sacking me. After all they said about giving me time to adjust...about it just being an informal interview...'

'Sacking you? But surely they can't do that?' Ross interrupted grimly.

Sarah shrugged. 'Well, it says in here that they're having to make cut-backs and, since I was the last teacher to be taken on, it follows that I'm the one they must ask to leave.'

'That's not being sacked,' Sally objected, but Sarah shook her head and asked her bitterly,

'Oh, no? What is it, then?'

Both her cousin and her husband tried to comfort and reassure her, but Sarah felt too miserable...too depressed, too much a failure almost, to be comforted.

'Well, at least that settles one thing, though,' Sally commented to her later when Ross had left for work. 'You'll have to accept Gray Philips's offer now.'

Have to? The words sent an icy chill racing down Sarah's spine. She wanted to protest, but the words just would not come. She felt too battered, too defeated to say anything. Self-pitying tears filled her eyes. She was a failure...who would employ her as a teacher now? How would it look on her CV to have to write that she had been sacked...or as good as?

Dark, despairing thoughts went round and round in her head. The last thing she wanted to do was to work for Gray Philips, and yet Sarah was right: what alternative did she have now? She could hardly expect to live on either her parents' or her cousins' charity while she spent potentially months and months looking for another job. Not when she had already been offered work.

No, Sally was right. No matter how much she might long for things to be different, she now had no alternative but to accept Gray Philips's offer.

CHAPTER FIVE

SARAH told Gray Philips as much later in the afternoon, conveying the news to him in a stilted, bitter little voice which did little to mask her true feelings.

Oddly, though, he did not seem inclined to question her lack of enthusiasm, saying only, 'Good, I'm glad that's settled, although we still have to discuss salary and time off. There's an empty room next to Robert's which has its own bathroom.'

Instantly Sarah stopped him.

'I can't live in,' she told him quickly. 'That's out of the question.'

He was frowning now.

'I'll undertake to stay with Robert if you have to work late,' she added before he could make any comment. 'But I cannot live in.'

He was watching her, she knew it, even though she could not bring herself to look directly at him. Was he going to ask her why not? She held her breath, praying that he wouldn't, not knowing what reason she could possibly give him that would make any sense; she only knew that she could not, for her own self-preservation, sleep under the same roof as this man.

She laughed bitterly at herself. Heavens, she sounded like someone out of a bad Victorian novel. What harm was sleeping under Gray Philips's roof going to do her? The harm that any kind of intimacy with him would bring her, she told herself miserably. The danger lay not in him, but in *her* awareness of him, and because of that... because of that it was absolutely essential that she did not allow herself to fall into the trap of daydreaming that sleeping under his roof meant that...

Meant that what? That it was only a short step from there to sleeping in his bed... in his arms. Pathetic. She was being completely pathetic.

'But if you do that you'll need a car,' he pointed out.

Sarah still didn't look at him. 'Yes, that's right. I was planning to buy one anyway,' she fibbed.

There was a long pause during which she prayed that he would say he had changed his mind and the job was no longer on offer, but to her shock he said instead, 'Well, I should have preferred you to live in for obvious reasons, but if you're insistent on not doing so I suppose I shall just have to accept it.'

She could hardly believe it. She turned her head, unwittingly allowing him to look straight into her eyes.

The grimly aware expression in his suggested that he was perfectly well aware of her reluctance to take the job, and she prayed that he was not also astute enough to work out *why* she was so reluctant to do so. But then, he couldn't be, could he? He couldn't have made it plainer that he was not looking for any kind of emotional involvement or commitment from any member of her sex, and surely, if he had suspected how vulnerable she was to him, he would have been the first to keep a very healthy distance between them. No, she was safe enough there. But if she ever had reason to fear that he *had* guessed how she felt... Well, then, she would have to leave, twelve months' contract or not.

He was talking about money now, and the salary he was prepared to pay her was more than generous.

As Sally told her later when he had gone, she would have been a fool to have turned him down.

She only wished she could be equally convinced.

Gray wanted her to start work for him immediately, but, as she explained to her cousin, she could not really do so until she had equipped herself with a car.

Immediately Sally offered generously, 'Why not use mine in the interim?'

But Sarah shook her head. 'No, I can't do that. It wouldn't be fair to you.'

If she had hoped to delay things by the need to acquire a suitable car she soon discovered that she had been living under a misapprehension, because that evening, just after they had finished dinner, the phone rang.

Ross went to answer it and came back ten minutes later to say, 'That was Gray Philips. It seems that he might have found you a suitable car. It certainly sounded quite a bargain. It's a private sale, only one owner, an older woman who rarely used it, so the mileage is very low.'

Sarah opened her mouth to object and point out to her cousin by marriage that Gray Philips had no right to take matters into his hands so arbitrarily and that she was perfectly capable of finding her own car, but before she could do so Ross continued

extolling the virtues of the second-hand model Gray
had found for her, and both he and Sally were so
enthusiastic and full of praise for what Gray Philips
had done that Sarah felt unable to express her true
feelings.

She was still smouldering with pent-up resentment when the three of them set out for the
nearby village, where the owner of the car apparently lived, half an hour later.

She told herself, as she sat seething in silence in
the back seat of the car, that nothing and no one
was going to manoeuvre her into buying a car she
had not chosen for herself, that she objected to
being treated like a child incapable of making her
own decisions, incapable of running her own life.

It was an attitude she maintained right up until
the moment she saw the car, clinging on to it even
in the face of Sally and Ross's enthusiasm and even
after having been introduced to its existing owner,
a charmingly vague widow in her late fifties, who
innocently answered one of the questions which had
been tugging at Sarah's mind by explaining that she
worked for Gray Philips as a member of his office
staff, and that it was when she had happened to
mention that she was thinking of changing her car
that he had announced that he knew of someone
who might be interested in buying it.

Yes, Laura Greig was undoubtedly genuine, and
at any other time Sarah would have been touched
by the way she referred to her car, almost as though
it possessed feelings and emotions rather than as
an inanimate object. However, because of the way
she felt that Gray Philips was trying to manipulate
her, to usurp her right to decide her own life, she

stubbornly clung on to her determination to reject the car.

That was, until she saw it.

She had no idea what she had actually expected—certainly, after meeting Laura Greig, she had had some vague notion that her car would turn out to be small and sturdy, and, while no doubt it would be immaculately maintained and carefully serviced, it would also be rather dull...beige or grey in colour most likely, and, even though she had never had any desire to own a vehicle that was either flashy in colour or fast, for some reason the fact that Gray Philips should decide that a car chosen by a very pleasant, but nevertheless rather staid widow in her late fifties would be suitable for her stirred up inside her the kind of rebellious feeling she could not remember feeling in years; certainly not since she had left her early teens behind.

To be confronted, therefore, by a shiny bright red convertible with cream leather seats, its hood folded back in the warmth of the late-evening sun, was such a shock that Sarah had to blink several times before she could actually really believe what she was seeing.

As she glanced from Laura Greig to the car and then back again she saw a faint flush colour the older woman's skin.

'My grandson helped me choose it,' she explained a little breathlessly. 'I wasn't so sure at first, but you know...' She touched the car's bodywork lovingly as she spoke, and then she added regretfully, 'My daughter's expected third baby turned out to be twins, and of course there's just no way

I can get all four children into Henrietta's back seat, so I'm afraid...' She gave a faint sigh.

Henrietta said nothing, merely standing four-square on the drive, her paintwork gleaming, but Sarah could have sworn that she wasn't regretting the loss of the four grandchildren as potential passengers.

'She *is* beautiful,' Sarah heard herself saying, and knew the instant she had spoken the words that she was lost.

Half an hour later, with the formalities complete, Sarah listened light-headedly as Laura Greig admitted, 'I know it's silly, but I'm so glad that Henrietta is going to a good home.' She flushed again. 'My son-in-law thinks I'm crazy... but she's the first car that's ever been just mine. While my husband was alive...' She gave a tiny sigh. 'When Gray described you to me as the ideal person to buy Henrietta from me, I wasn't so sure. In fact, right up until the moment I met you I was quite sure I was going to have to tell you that I'd changed my mind.'

Sarah listened to her, trying not to allow herself to wonder if Gray Philips, beneath his outwardly insensitive manner, was not perhaps a far better student of human nature than she had actually realised.

Later, when they were driving home, Sally commented, 'Gray Philips must think an awful lot of you, Sarah. I mean, to go to all that trouble for you...'

'I don't think it's that he has a particularly high opinion of *me*...more that he's at his wits' end to

know what to do with his son,' Sarah corrected her
wryly.

'Mm.'

Sally didn't sound totally convinced, but Sarah
resolutely refused to allow herself to be seduced into
the folly of deceiving herself that Sally was right.
After all, she had had ample evidence of exactly
how Gray Philips viewed her, and she knew quite
well that, if Robbie hadn't formed such an instant
and strong attachment to her, Gray would never
have considered employing her.

Since it was going to be a full twenty-four hours
at least before Sarah could take legal possession of
the car, and get it taxed and insured, Sally insisted
that, rather than delay starting her new job, she
must borrow her car. Unwillingly Sarah accepted
her generous offer, knowing that, little as she
wanted to start work for Gray, for Robbie's sake
she could not delay doing so.

It was the good manners instilled in her as a child
that forced her to telephone Gray Philips once they
had returned to the cottage.

When he answered its ring just as she was about
to replace the receiver she stifled the mingled
feelings of panic and delight that flooded her to say
in an unnaturally stilted voice, 'I hope I haven't
disturbed you, but I just wanted to thank you for
going to so much trouble on my behalf with the
car.'

'You've been to see it, then.' Unlike hers, his
voice was firm and free of any hesitance. 'That's
good. Did you like it?'

His question surprised her, especially after the
high-handed way in which he had virtually ordered

her to go and view the car in the first place. Caught
off guard, she responded honestly and enthusi-
astically. 'Yes...yes, I did, although it wasn't quite
what I expected.'

She stopped, angry with herself for being betrayed into so much enthusiasm, but Gray appeared not to have noticed, because all he said was
a casual, 'Well, I'm glad that's settled. You'll be
here in the morning, then?'

Sarah took a deep breath. 'Yes,' she agreed.
'What time would you like me to arrive?'

'Well, I generally leave around eight. If you could
be here for then ... It's early, I know. But I like to
be at the factory for half-past. Mrs Jacobs used to
give Robert his breakfast, and...'

'Of course, I'll make sure that he's properly fed,'
Sarah started to assure him grittily, but he stopped
her, surprising her when he told her coolly,

'Yes, I'm sure you will. However, what I was
going to say was that, in view of the fact that you'll
have such an early start, it might be best if you had
your own breakfast with Robert. That is unless you
have the same deep-rooted objection to eating in
the house as you appear to have about sleeping in
it.'

Sarah didn't know what to say. She could hear
the sarcasm in his voice very clearly, and it made
her cringe. He was making her sound like some kind
of fictional Victorian spinster, the type who would
have refused to sit on a chair previously occupied
by a man.

When she thought she had her own voice safely
under control she responded as neutrally as she
could.

'Thank you. I agree it would be much easier all round if I had my meals with Robert, although, of course, in that case there will have to be some adjustment in my salary too——'

The explosive sound of derision he made silenced her.

'Look, I'm not going to argue with you about the cost of a few bits of food. From the look of you I suspect you probably eat less than Robert anyway. Women! When will you ever learn that no man ever equated thinness with desirability? A woman who is confident and happy about her natural shape, who enjoys her food and shows it, is far, far more attractive than some neurotic female who's constantly worrying about her weight and picking at her meals...'

Sarah inhaled sharply and then held her breath while mentally counting to ten. 'There is nothing wrong with my appetite,' she told him shortly. 'And if I'm a little on the thin side it's due more to stress and worry—of the threat of losing my job—rather than any desire to starve myself in order to impress some man.'

'I'm glad to hear it,' Gray told her smoothly. 'I don't want Robert adding unhealthy and potentially dangerous eating habits to all his other emotional problems.'

'If you really thought I was likely to do that I'm surprised you wanted to employ me,' Sarah countered sharply.

There was silence from his end that went on for so long that she actually began to think he must have hung up on her, and then, just as she was about to put her own receiver down in reciprocal

irritation, he told her quietly, 'It isn't *my* opinion
of you that's important, but Robert's, and besides...' He stopped speaking as Sarah heard quite
clearly the sound of his doorbell ringing. 'I'm afraid
I have to go. I'll expect you in the morning, then,
at eight. Goodbye, Sarah.'

She discovered as she replaced the receiver that
she was trembling inside. When she closed her eyes
in angry self-disgust they immediately stung with
sharp tears.

What was the matter with her? If she hadn't
known it already, that biting little exchange must
have warned her how antagonistic he was towards
her, how little he liked her, never mind desired her,
and yet just because she had spoken with him she
was reacting like a child who had just been given
its heart's desire.

Thank God she wasn't going to be living in. She
tried to envisage coming down to breakfast in the
morning with Robert and finding him already there,
drinking coffee and reading his paper... perhaps
wearing some kind of towelling robe, his legs bare,
his body still damp from the shower.

The physical desire flooding her body shocked
her mind and bruised her emotions. She had never
seen herself in this light before, never known she
was capable of such uninvited sexual awareness...

Would never have believed herself capable of
such explicit mental visualisation, even to the extent
that... She took a deep breath and then another,
trying to subdue her rioting thoughts.

Mindful of the early start she would need in the
morning, she went to bed early, but she only slept
fitfully and was awake long before her alarm went

off, in the end abandoning the folly of lying there waiting for it to ring, and instead getting up and going downstairs to make herself a cup of coffee before going back upstairs to get showered and dressed.

She dressed, bearing in mind the nature of her new job, pulling on a pair of culotte-type shorts in practical cotton, wearing them with a matching brightly coloured T-shirt, and then adding a sweatshirt in case the day proved to be cooler than the clear blue sky suggested.

On her feet she wore a pair of well-worn canvas shoes, and into the large bag she was taking with her she had put a plentiful supply of papers, pencils and a notebook, so that once she had elucidated from Robbie just what stage he was up to educationally she could set about drawing up a suitable programme in order that she could teach him while at the same time ensuring that he was enjoying himself.

Although Gray had stipulated that she had to sign a contract ensuring that she would remain in his employ for a full year, he had not said what he expected her to do once Robbie went to school at the beginning of the new term. Of course, he would expect her to take Robbie to school and then to collect him in the afternoon and to remain with him until he himself returned from work, but what about the time in between? Was she to take total charge of Robbie's life as though she were in fact a substitute mother... buy his clothes, wash and iron them, be there in case there were any problems at school? They were only just into the school holiday, she reminded herself, and there was plenty of time for her to ascertain exactly what Gray Philips had in mind. One thing was certain: he was not the type of man to be reluctant to tell her exactly what it was he wanted and expected from her.

It was ten to eight when she arrived, and, having carefully parked Sally's car so that it did not obstruct Gray Philips's exit, she made her way to the house.

While she was hesitating about whether to ring the front doorbell or go round to the back door the front door opened, and Gray Philips was standing there, beckoning her inside.

Instead of the towelling robe of her imaginings, he was wearing a dark navy suit and a crisp white shirt, together with a soberly striped tie, and yet she had to confess as she walked into the house that his effect on her senses was just as powerful and erotic as though he had been far less formally dressed.

What was it about the sight of a tall, broad-shouldered man wearing a dark expensive suit as casually as though it were a pair of jeans that was so instantly compelling and so instantly... so instantly sexy?

Perhaps the answer lay in Gray's assurance and self-confidence, in the fact that he was wearing such formal clothes so carelessly and easily.

As she hesitated, not sure if she was to walk straight through into the kitchen or not, he closed the front door.

As she automatically turned round she saw he was looking at her, one eyebrow lifting as he studied her casual clothes.

Immediately she said defensively, 'You didn't say that you wanted me to wear a uniform. I'm not a trained nanny, and I thought Robbie would feel more comfortable with me...more relaxed if...'

'If you looked like a teenager rather than an adult,' he supplied mockingly.

A teenager. He was being ridiculous, and if he was trying to imply that her clothes were too young for her...but then, to her shock, as she glowered at him he added softly, 'Mind you, it's just as well he is so young. With those legs...'

The long, lingering appraisal he gave the lower half of her body was so unexpected, so totally at variance with his previous attitude towards her, that she could only stand there, her face bright red, her eyes flashing with indignation. Quite what she would have said to him if the kitchen door hadn't opened and Robbie hadn't come hurtling towards her, to virtually fling himself into her arms, she had no idea, but by the time she had bent down to catch the little boy, lifting him up into her arms while she said hello to him, her anger had gone, melted away by the touching delight of Robbie's pleasure in seeing her.

'Believe me now, do you?' Gray was saying to his son as Robbie wrapped his arms round Sarah's neck, refusing to let go of her.

Darting a quick glance at Gray, Sarah saw that his eyes were shadowed and that he quickly averted his face from her, as though he didn't want her looking directly at him.

Ross had said that originally Gray had fought desperately to retain custody of his son. If he cared for the little boy at all it must have hurt him dread-

fully to have been turned into a complete stranger
to him...a stranger, moreover, whom Robbie so
obviously disliked and feared.

'My father says that you're going to look after
me, that you're going to be here *every* day,' Robbie
was saying to her, although Sarah's heart ached over
that formal, stilted 'my father' when he should still
have been saying 'Daddy'.

'Yes, that's right, Robbie,' she confirmed, while
beside her Gray frowned and told her curtly,

'Give him to me, he's too heavy for you.'

Too heavy for her? Sarah was about to deny that
she was so feeble that she couldn't carry the weight
of a six-year-old, and an almost too thin six-year-
old at that, when she reminded herself that Gray
was Robbie's father, and that for Robbie's sake one
of her tasks while she was here with him must be
to build some bridges between father and son so
that Robbie could develop the trust and love in his
sole parent that every child needed to have if they
were to thrive and develop emotionally.

However, as she started to pass Robbie over to
Gray, the little boy tightened his arms around her,
his body going stiff with denial of what she was
doing.

'I've brought some paper with me, Robbie,' she
told him cheerfully, ignoring the pleading look in
his eyes as Gray took him from her. 'And
tomorrow, if you like, we can go shopping and buy
some coloured pencils.'

'Today. I want to go today,' Robbie told her, but
Sarah shook her head and repeated firmly,

'I'm afraid not, Robbie. Until I get my new car
we won't be able to go out because the one I'm

using at the moment doesn't have any rear seatbelts
in it.'

That had been one of the things she had been
most insistent upon when she had decided to pur-
chase her shiny bright red convertible. Rear seatbelts were a must if she was going to feel
comfortable with Robbie as a passenger.

'But we'll find plenty of things to do today,' she
told him with a smile, asking, 'Have you had your
breakfast yet?'

When he shook his head she suggested, 'Then
why don't we let your fa...daddy go to work? Then
you can have something to eat and you and I can
decide what we're going to do today.'

As she spoke Gray was already heading for the
kitchen; Sarah followed him, her attention immediately focusing on the large wooden kitchen
table with its half a dozen chairs, the table, like the
kitchen, designed to accommodate the needs of a
busy and close family, and yet all that was on it
was a solitary mug of coffee and a half-eaten piece
of toast on a plate.

For some reason the sight of that single mug and
plate made her ache inside. How could she blame
Gray Philips for his attitude towards her sex? He
had presumably loved Robbie's mother when he
married her, had expected to share with her all the
pleasure and closeness of a warm family unit, instead of which his wife had been consistently un-
faithful to him before leaving him and taking with
her his child.

Gray had already put Robbie down on the floor,
and instantly the little boy came and pressed close
to Sarah's side.

'I've had a spare set of keys cut for you,' Gray told her, reaching into his pocket and then handing them over to her. As he did so his fingers brushed accidentally against her wrist, causing her to tense and withdraw quickly from the physical contact. Her flesh tingled where he had touched it, an odd, insidious sensation of heat and weakness creeping up her arm.

'I should be back for six this evening.' He was frowning, his mind already elsewhere, and just for a moment Sarah weakly gave in to the desire to ask herself what it would be like if she were married to him, if Robbie were her child. Would he leave her with a cursory peck on the cheek, a distant promise to try not to be late, or would he, as the fullness of his lower lip seemed to suggest, allow a more sensual side of his nature full rein in the privacy of his own home? Would he kiss her tenderly and lingeringly, give her the kind of kiss that would stay with her all day, an implicit promise of a different kind of shared intimacy to come later in the day once Robbie was asleep and they were on their own?

With a tiny shock Sarah recognised that her body was already responding wantonly to the erotic stimulus of her dangerous thoughts. Beside her Gray reached for his coffee, grimacing in distaste as he realised it had gone cold.

Leaving both it and his toast unfinished, he picked up the briefcase standing on the floor beside the chair.

For a moment before he headed for the door he hesitated and looked at Robbie, and, although Sarah silently willed him to make some gesture of affection and warmth towards his son, he made no

move to approach him, saying only with curt
sternness, 'Now remember, Robert, behave
yourself,' and then he was gone, his footsteps
echoing across the wooden floor of the hall before
the front door closed behind him.

'Sarah...Sarah, I'm hungry.'

Robbie was tugging at her sleeve, looking up at
her. His mouth was exactly like his father's, Sarah
recognised with a small pang as she smiled back at
him and asked him what he would like to eat.

CHAPTER SIX

A WEEK passed, and, although she and Robbie had very quickly established an excellent relationship, Sarah felt as though she had done nothing to improve the relationship between Robbie and Gray. But then, how could she when Robbie saw so little of his father? On several occasions Gray had returned later than he had planned, having rung her from the factory to say that he was going to be delayed and asking her if she could possibly stay on, so that she was the one who put Robbie to bed and who read him his bedtime story.

She could tell that Gray was irritated by her refusal to live in, but she was determined to stick to her decision. Seeing him in the morning, standing beside the kitchen table in shirt-sleeves, quickly gulping the half-cold mug of coffee that seemed to be the only breakfast he had, was enough to make her so achingly and wantonly aware of him that she knew she was far too vulnerable to risk actually living in the same house with him. And yet why should she feel this way about him? He had certainly not given her any encouragement to do so, and she had never thought of herself as being so highly sexually motivated that she could ever succumb to such an acute attack of a desire and need that was purely physical. Which meant...
Which meant what? That she had fallen in love with him? At her age? Surely she was beyond that kind

of folly? Falling in love was something that belonged to extreme youth. With maturity and experience came the knowledge that real love was something that grew slowly and sometimes painfully; that it was a delicate plant that needed careful nurturing... And besides... besides, her feelings went deeper than mere sexual excitement and the adoration of some out-of-reach mythical male on to whose real character she had grafted a whole host of ideological and impossible attributes. In the morning, when she watched Gray grimacing over his cold coffee... when she saw the way Robbie turned away from him and to her, she ached inside for him. In the evening, when he came back from work looking drained and tense, she wanted to comfort him, to share his burden with him, to open her arms to him and hold him in much the same way as she did Robbie, to pour out over him the loving tenderness of her instinctive emotional response to his need, and then he would move, say or do something that would make her so aware of him as a man that immediately and dramatically her feelings would change, becoming so intensely sensual and keen-pitched that the ache inside her body was an embarrassment and an anguish to her.

This was not being 'in love'. This was love itself, this complex and uncomfortable mixture of emotions and needs that common sense and logic told her she had no right and no reason to feel, but which still persisted in growing inside her. But how could she love him when he was still in so many ways a stranger to her? The intimacy of being in someone's home for so many hours of the day of necessity laid many aspects of their lives open, but

these were only domestic details, like the fact that
he ironed his own shirts and did his own
washing...like the fact that he seemed to have little
or no idea what size clothes his son took, and,
although he had bought Robbie new clothes immediately that he had come to live with him, to
replace those which he was rapidly outgrowing,
none of them really seemed to be the right size, nor
really suitable for a child living in the country and
surrounded by a large garden. Robbie needed tough
outdoor clothes, sensible tracksuits, T-shirts and
shorts, not the dull, old-fashioned things that were
all she could find in his wardrobe. Robbie needed
a mother, she acknowledged, warning herself that
she must never allow herself to fall into the trap of
letting Robbie see her in that light, for his sake even
more than her own. While she was an adult, and
therefore technically at least capable of knowing
the pain she was ultimately inflicting on herself,
Robbie was still only a child. She could not...must
not allow him to become so attached to her that
when she eventually left he would suffer.

She did as much as she could, casually mentioning his father during their conversations,
making it so that it was as though Gray was very
much a part of Robbie's life, even if Robbie himself
stubbornly refused to admit him into it.

Today was her birthday, and tonight Sally and
Ross were taking her out for a meal. There had been
cards on the breakfast table at the cottage for her
this morning and both Sally and Ross had got up
especially early to be there with her while she
opened them.

When she left she contrasted the warmth of affection that existed within her own family with the loneliness of Robbie's family life. Her parents had sent her a card and a long loving letter; there were cards from her brother and his family in Canada, from cousins and aunts and uncles, from old school and university friends now scattered all over the country and Europe in different jobs; and this evening she had the treat of being taken out to dinner at a very special and expensive local restaurant to look forward to.

At the weekend, when she had not worked, as Gray had been at home to look after Robbie himself, Sally had dragged her off to their nearest town, where she had insisted on buying her a new dress, despite Sarah's protest that it was far too expensive.

'I'm being well paid for this latest commission,' Sally had told her, adding with a grin, 'Besides, it makes me feel less guilty about my own extravagance. What do you think Ross will think of this?' she had asked Sarah, parading for her inspection in an extremely slinky black jersey dress with tiny shoe-string straps.

'I think if you wear it when we go out for my birthday he'll be wishing me a million miles away by the time we go home,' Sarah had told her frankly.

It had worried her at first, that her presence might become an irritation to her cousin's husband, causing friction between husband and wife, but, as Sally had assured her, Ross was far too easygoing a husband for that kind of thing. 'Besides,' she had added with one of her familiar grins, 'the internal

walls of the cottage are a couple of feet thick, and
you know yourself how impossible it is even to hear
the phone ring from one room to another, so if
Ross wants to make mad, passionate love to me...'
She had broken off to laugh at the expression on
Sarah's face, teasing her, 'I'd forgotten how easily
embarrassed you are. Besides, from what I've
heard, having adults sharing your roof with you is
nothing. It's once you've got children running
around and bursting into your bedroom at pre-
cisely the wrong moment that you really begin to
understand frustration.'

This time both of them laughed.

After her weekend away from him Robbie was
tending to cling to her, wanting constant reassurance that she was not going to go away,
wanting plenty of cuddles and confirmation of her
physical affection for him. He was a very loving
little boy, although, from what Sarah could gather
from his comments about his mother and the life
he had lived with his grandmother, his mother had
never been particularly loving towards him.

Sarah had noticed how worried he was about
touching her with sticky fingers, and how he sometimes tensed a little as though half expecting her
rejection. His mother, she had learned from his
innocent chatter, had had long pink nails and
always worn high-heeled shoes. Perhaps unfairly,
Sarah acknowledged, she was beginning to get the
impression that Gray's ex-wife had been far from
the devoted mother she had pretended to be... a
woman who had preferred to leave her son in his

grandmother's charge, so that she was free to live the life of a single woman.

Reminding herself that life could be extremely difficult for single parents, who should never be expected to devote every single second of their lives to their children, Sarah tried hard not to pass judgement on Robbie's mother.

One thing the woman most definitely had done, though, was to instil in Robbie a very definite fear and rejection of his father. Sarah only had to mention Gray's name for Robbie to tense, screwing up his face, although he had for the first time on Friday evening, when Gray had been late, commented to her, 'I'm glad that Daddy's working late because it means that you'll stay with me for longer, doesn't it?'

It was the first time he had referred to Gray as 'Daddy', and gave Sarah hope that she might in time help him to overcome his antipathy towards his father.

This morning Gray had told her that he intended to come home early, and so she had not, as she had originally intended, told him that because she was going out to dinner she would need to leave on time at six, but it was now a quarter-past six and there was no sign of him, and when she had rung the factory there had not been anyone there to answer the telephone.

Now, gnawing her bottom lip, she looked at the clock and decided that she would hang on until seven before ringing Sally to warn her that she might not be able to make it in time.

In the end it was ten-past seven when she
eventually picked up the receiver to dial her cousin's
number.

Sally answered the phone straight away.

'Oh, no!' she exclaimed when Sarah told her that
Gray wasn't back. 'Didn't you explain to him this
morning that we were going out?'

'No,' Sarah admitted. 'He said he would be back
early. I've tried the factory and there's no reply,
and, of course, I can't leave Robbie on his own.'

'No, of course not,' Sally agreed. 'The table's
booked for half-eight . . . and I doubt if we can get
them to change it. The restaurant is very popular.'

'Look, if I can't get back in time there's no reason
why you and Ross shouldn't go by yourselves,'
Sarah told her.

'Sarah, this is your birthday treat,' Sally reminded her. 'Oh, drat the man! What does he think
you are? To not even have the courtesy to ring you
and let you know . . .'

'He's normally very good about that,' Sarah
found herself defending Gray. 'Look, I'll give it to
half-past seven, and if he isn't back by then I'll ring
you and let you know.'

Half-past seven. Robbie's bedtime arrived
without any sign of Gray. Sighing to herself, Sarah
rang her cousin. Sally was very forthright, and
rather angry about the situation, but accepted that
Sarah had no option other than to stay with Robbie.

'I hope you let Gray know how unfair he's being,'
Sally told her, assuring Sarah that she and Ross
would go on ahead without her so that the evening
wasn't completely wasted. 'Although it seems very

unfair, since it was your birthday we were supposed to be celebrating.'

Having soothed her cousin, Sarah turned to find Robbie standing a few feet away from her, his face puckered with anxiety.

It hurt her so much that he should be so afraid...so vulnerable...so aware of how very unreliable adult promises, adult love could be. She picked him up wordlessly, hugging him to reassure him, and then said cheerfully, 'Come on, Robbie, bath-time.'

'May I have a piece of cake for supper?' he asked her, his frown turning to smiles.

Sarah shook her head. She and Robbie had spent the morning making a birthday cake which they had eaten with due ceremony at teatime.

'No cake at bedtime, Robbie,' she reminded him. 'How about a lovely crisp apple instead?'

Solemnly he nodded his head. He was such a biddable, obedient child...too biddable and quiet at times, she reflected, watching him.

Of course, the fact that he had been brought up in his grandmother's household was probably partially responsible for that, and there was, after all, nothing wrong with good, old-fashioned manners, but in Robbie's case a little more exuberance, a little less tension and apprehension, would make it far easier for him to adjust when the time came for him to start his new school. Sarah was afraid that the robust company of other children of his own age might prove too overwhelming for him and send him right back into his shell. She had already been making enquiries to ascertain if there were any out-of-school activities he could take part in which would enable him to meet other children of his age, and this week she was taking him swimming at a time when she had found out that other children were likely to be at the local sports centre.

By eight o'clock Robbie was bathed and in bed. Sarah read him his favourite story before he went to sleep. She had noticed that whenever he was stressed or upset he tended to fall back on the security of needing the familiar to comfort him. Slowly she was trying to widen his horizons, to help him become less apprehensive and insecure, but it would be a long, slow process... something that could not be accomplished quickly. Something which might do more harm than good when the time eventually came for her to leave him. Would he see her then as yet another adult who was deserting him?

Sighing to herself, Sarah went back downstairs, taking his dirty clothes with her to put them in the washing-machine.

Since she had no option but to await Gray's return home, she might as well find something useful with which to occupy her time.

In the kitchen, the buddleia she and Robbie had picked from the garden provided a rich splash of colour on the pine table, even though the flowers were beginning to fall already. Robbie had a surprisingly well-developed eye for a child so young and had produced a very passable drawing of the flowers. She had pinned it to the notice-board she had put up in the kitchen, again with Robbie's help, although she had asked Gray's permission first before doing so. He had raised his eyebrows a little but had made no comment other than, 'Well, if you think it's necessary.'

Not necessary, perhaps, but useful. Every teatime she and Robbie made a list of all the things they had done and all the things they wanted to do, and both lists were duly pinned up on the board. Robbie could read quite well, but his maths was poor. and Sarah was trying to improve it by getting him to add up both lists every day, subtracting one total from the other, turning the learning exercise into a game which both of them enjoyed.

At ten o'clock, just as she was finishing the last of the ironing, she heard Gray's car, and saw the security lights come on as he walked towards the house.

He came straight into the kitchen via the back door instead of using the front door. It had been a warm day, the atmosphere a little heavy, and outside the summer evening air was still warm.

Gray had removed his jacket and his tie. The top buttons of his shirt were unfastened, his skin looked slightly damp, and there was a dark growth of beard along his jaw.

He was, Sarah saw, frowning, and the kitchen light revealed taut lines of tension beside his eyes and alongside his mouth.

As always the sight of him reactivated all the aching awareness she fought so hard to control when he wasn't there. He smelled faintly of heat and sweat, and the knowledge that he was so male and human was like a powerful kick in her stomach, a wrenching, agonising tide of reaction that made her tense every muscle in her body.

His frown deepened as he saw what she was doing, as though for some reason such domestic intimacy displeased him.

'Robbie asleep?' he asked her as he put down his briefcase and pulled out one of the kitchen chairs, dropping wearily into it.

'Yes,' Sarah confirmed.

'I won't go up and disturb him, then.'

Sarah compressed her lips. If it was hard getting Robbie to see his father as someone he could love and grow close to then it was almost equally hard getting Gray to acknowledge his responsibility to give Robbie the encouragement and affection he needed to be able to overthrow his antipathy towards him.

'I'm sorry I'm so late,' Gray was apologising. 'A crisis blew up with one of our suppliers. I had to go to London to get it sorted out. I told Mary to ring and let you know I'd be back around eight, I know, but unfortunately things took longer than I'd anticipated.'

Mary was his secretary, a woman in her late thirties. It was pointless now telling him that not only had she not received his message, but also that she had had other plans for the evening.

Since she had finished the ironing and there was no reason for her to stay, she picked up her handbag from the dresser, checking that she had got her car keys.

As she headed for the door she heard Gray opening the fridge door behind her.

'What's this?' he demanded, removing what was left of the birthday cake. At Robbie's insistence she had iced on it the message 'Happy Birthday, Sarah'.

'It's a cake,' she told him stiffly, feeling somehow vulnerable and defensive.

'So today is your birthday.' He was looking at her in an oddly speculative way that made her flush without knowing why she should do so. 'I should have thought a woman of your age would have had far more exciting plans for celebrating such an occasion than eating home-made birthday cake with a six-year-old.'

The cynical tone of his voice and the way his mouth twisted combined to fuel her own resentment and pain.

'As a matter of fact, I should have been going out to dinner,' she told him angrily. 'However, since I neither had your message from Mary, nor felt able to leave Robbie on his own, and since you had assured me this morning that you would be back early——'

'You had a date?'

Why did he make it sound such an impossibility? Did he realise how insulting... how unkind he was being? Not for anything now would she tell him that her date had been with her cousin and her husband. Instead she told him stiffly, 'Yes, I did.'

She waited for him to apologise... to tell her that he was sorry if he had spoilt her evening, but instead he said cynically, 'Well, no doubt by keeping him dangling you'll have made him even keener for your company. Isn't that how the female mind works?'

Sarah glared at him, her love for him overwhelmed by anger at what he was implying.

'I can't speak for other women,' she told him acidly. 'But mine most certainly does not, and now, if you'll excuse me, I'll say goodnight.'

She was still fuming when she reached the cottage, all in darkness because Sally and Ross had gone out without her. In the sitting-room her cards were lined up on the mantelpiece and the window-sill, a reminder of how happily she had started the day. Damn Gray Philips...just because his wife had been the sort of woman who enjoyed manipulating and hurting people there was no need for him to accuse her... She stopped herself. She was taking things far too personally...far, far too personally...becoming far too emotionally involved, not just with Robbie but with Gray himself as well, while he barely knew she existed.

Tiredly she went upstairs and prepared for bed.

'So you told him just how annoyed you were, then?' Sally was demanding.

'Sort of,' Sarah agreed, unwilling to explain just what had happened.

'You mustn't let him take advantage of your kind heart, you know, Sarah. You're employed to take charge of Robbie, not to act as a surrogate mother.'

Sarah sighed. 'I've got to go,' she told her cousin. 'Otherwise I'm going to be late.'

There was nothing unusual in the sight of Gray's car parked outside when she arrived at the house half an hour later, although it was odd to walk into the kitchen to find it empty and the lights left on.

A plate with a cold and unappetising piece of half-eaten pizza on it was on the kitchen table with a half-drunk mug of coffee.

Frowning, Sarah opened the door from the kitchen into the hall.

Silence. For a moment she wasn't sure what she ought to do. She felt rather like someone boarding the abandoned *Mary Celeste* must have felt, she reflected as she hesitated. The sensible thing to do was to go upstairs and find out if Robbie was still in bed, but she hadn't forgotten the way Gray had looked at her when he had thought she was rifling through his desk, and, besides, if he *had* overslept, as seemed the case...

The thought of accidentally confronting him, perhaps half naked as he emerged from his bedroom or bathroom——

Stop it, she warned herself firmly, ignoring her emotional vulnerability and heading for the stairs.

She was an employee... paid to take charge of Robbie... and that was what she must do. If Gray had overslept... Well, she could always send Robbie in to wake up his father, she told herself as she reached the landing and opened the door into Robbie's room.

The curtains were still drawn. There was no sign of Robbie, but she could hear water running in his bathroom, though it wasn't that that held her rooted to the floor just inside the doorway. No, it was the sight of Gray himself, lying sprawled on Robbie's bed, still fully dressed and fast asleep.

As she stared at him Robbie emerged from his bathroom, semi-dressed.

'I had a bad dream,' he told her in a whisper. 'Daddy came upstairs. He said that I wasn't to be afraid because he was there.'

At any other time Sarah would have rejoiced in
the natural, easy way Robbie had called Gray
'Daddy', in the way he seemed to accept that when
Gray said 'don't be afraid', there was nothing to
fear...just as she would have rejoiced in the fact
that Gray had heard his son cry out and had responded to that cry.

'I'm hungry, Sarah. I want my breakfast,' she
heard Robbie saying as he opened the bedroom
door and headed for the stairs.

She was just about to call him back so that she
could get him to wake Gray up when Gray himself
moved, turning over, frowning in his sleep as he
tried to make himself comfortable in the too small
bed.

He must have been exhausted to be able to sleep
at all in that confined space, especially when he
was sharing it with Robbie, Sarah reflected,
stepping back towards the door, expecting at any
moment that he would open his eyes, but instead
he flung out his arm, and in doing so knocked over
the covered glass of cordial and water she always
left for Robbie.

Sarah reacted instinctively, darting forward, too
late to do anything other than rescue the glass from
the damp carpet, but it was while she was kneeling
on the floor beside the bed that she suddenly felt
Gray's hand touch her hair.

The total unexpectedness of it turned her rigid,
unable to move...unable to breathe...unable to
do anything. His fingers moved slowly against her
scalp. He made a deep, soft sound of pleasure,
before coiling his hand round her hair and tugging
it gently as he urged her down towards him.

His eyes, she saw, were still closed, and he was
in effect still fast asleep, totally unconscious of what
he was doing. Which meant...which meant that
she had to remove his hand from her hair right away
and then wake him up. Heaven alone knew who he
thought she was. Some unknown woman with
whom he had had the kind of intimate relationship
that...

She swallowed hard. She was so close to him now
that she could see the pores of his skin, the dark
growth of his beard, the silky curl of his eyelashes.
She could smell the warm male heat of his body,
and instinctively, to prevent herself from overbal-
ancing, she had unwittingly placed her hand on his
chest so that beneath her palm she could feel the
heavy, slightly uneven thud of his heartbeat.

'Mm...' Her own heart pounded as he nuzzled
the soft skin of her throat, his thumb stroking
rhythmically behind her ear. Her senses were overwhelmed by a fierce flood of sensation, her nipples
tightening...swelling, her whole body shockingly
responsive to his touch. His beard rasped roughly
against her tender skin and yet the sensation was
more erotic than unpleasant, sending tiny shivers
of pleasure darting under her skin. Instinctively she
moved closer to him, arching her throat so that his
mouth could caress it. The hand she had placed on
his chest tightened, her fingers curling. She could
hear the sound of her own uneven breathing, could
feel how her body trembled and ached.

She was wearing a thin cotton top and a pair of
shorts, and when Gray's free hand cupped her
breast she gave a small, startled gasp of shock, but
he was oblivious to it, his eyes still closed, his mouth

still nuzzling her throat, his tongue-tip stroking it,
his teeth gently dragging exquisite trails of pleasure
over it.

Sarah trembled against him, knowing that she
should pull away from him, and yet somehow or
other the message she gave her body to do so
became either confused or ignored, so that instead
of pulling away she was doing exactly the opposite
and was in fact pushing herself closer and closer
into his intimate embrace . . . her body wantonly ignoring the frantic messages from her brain to move
away from him before it was too late, before he
woke up and realised what he was doing, what she
was allowing him, *encouraging* him, almost, to do.

She shivered as his thumb stroked slowly against
her nipple, swallowing the small moan of pleasure
that bubbled in her throat. His mouth dragged
erotically against her skin, seeking her lips, and she
couldn't stop herself from turning her head so that
he could find them.

When he did so her heart jerked to a standstill,
her senses sent into a dizzy frenzy by the urgent
caress of his mouth against her lips.

This was no tentative, seeking kiss, but the kind
of kiss a man gave a woman whom he intimately
and passionately desired.

But who was that woman? Not her, Sarah acknowledged, going still in his hold, her desire suddenly chilled and cold, her body stiff with anguished
shame and rejection.

Gray was still kissing her, his teeth biting sharply
into her bottom lip as he sensed her resistance.

The unexpectedness of that sharp pain made her
cry out and jerk back from him.

Instantly his eyes opened, a frown drawing his eyebrows together as he stared at her.

Frantically Sarah scrambled to her feet, stammering in panic, 'You knocked over Robbie's water glass. I'm sorry if I woke you.'

He was still frowning, and she could almost feel him thinking... trying to catch hold of an elusive memory, a troublesome vague awareness.

He was, she realised, focusing on her bottom lip. Instantly she caught hold of it between her teeth, trying not to wince as the broken skin stung, her heart pounding heavily in her ears. She felt sick... vulnerable... so afraid that he might remember and blame her... so afraid that he might think that *she* had been the one... that he might guess... but when he spoke he demanded irritably, 'What the hell am I doing in here?' making it clear that he had no memory of what had happened, and freeing her to say unsteadily,

'Robbie said he had a bad dream and that you came up to him. You must have fallen asleep with him.'

Gray gave a grunt, which might have been an assent or might not. He swung his legs on to the floor, cursing under his breath as he complained, 'God, my back.'

Sarah was already backing towards the door. His movements had dragged his shirt out of his trousers, revealing the taut male flesh of his abdomen and chest. He stretched and she heard his bones crack.

'What time is it?' he asked her, cursing again when she told him. 'Hell, I've got a meeting in half an hour. I'll have to ring Mary and get it delayed.'

He was still frowning, his thoughts quite obviously on his work, nothing in his manner to suggest that he was remotely aware of what had happened, and yet as she opened the bedroom door he looked straight at her, his gaze searching her face before dropping to her mouth.

Inside she was trembling so violently that she was surprised he couldn't see it. Her bottom lip was still clenched between her teeth, the pain from her torn flesh increasing with every second, but she dared not let him look at her bitten lip and remember.

Opening the door, she turned round and hurried through it. Downstairs Robbie had helped himself to his cereal. There was a milk moustache around his mouth, and he looked up, giving Sarah a wide beaming smile as she walked into the kitchen.

She had her back to the door half an hour later when Gray walked into the kitchen. Immediately she tensed, unable to turn round and look at him. Had he realised... remembered... or had he been so deeply asleep that he had no recollection of having touched her... kissed her?

She heard him open the fridge door and she forced herself to turn round. Her heart was thumping violently with anxiety and pain; he looked so remote, so distant... looking at him now in all the formality of his dark-clothed suit, it was almost impossible to believe that he had... She swallowed, reminding herself that it had not been she he had been making love to; that it had not been she whom he had kissed and caressed.

He had removed some orange juice from the fridge and was about to turn round. Immediately she busied herself, fussing over Robbie.

'Are we going to have some more birthday cake today, Sarah?' Robbie was asking her.

Sarah knew that Gray was watching her, studying her, and, even though she could feel the slow crawl of hot colour seeping up over her throat and face, she refused to turn her own head and look at him. It was like having to resist an actual physical force, she recognised as she fought her own powerful desire to turn her head and see why he was watching her so closely.

Ten minutes later, having finished his own breakfast, Gray picked up his briefcase and headed for the door, pausing only to say curtly to her, 'If you've got a moment, please, Sarah.'

Numbly she followed him out into the hall. He had remembered after all. And he was going to demand to know why she had not stopped him... why she had not woken him, why she——

'I think it would be a good idea if Robbie was to abstain from eating any more birthday cake,' he told her. 'I suspect that was probably the cause of the bad dream that kept both him and me awake last night.'

Sarah focused on him and heard him continuing critically, 'I really would have thought you would have had more sense than to allow him to eat such stuff anyway... all that sugar and fat...'

'I used a low-fat sugar-free recipe,' Sarah informed him stiffly.

How dared he imply that *she* was responsible for Robbie's nightmare when he...? It was on the tip

of her tongue to point out that, if he really was
concerned about Robbie's bad dreams, he could
find the cause of them far closer to home than
looking for it in her cooking, but the shock of his
unfair criticism when she had been expecting him
to raise a very different subject indeed was numbing
her brain so much that she couldn't get her tongue
round the words she wanted to say.

As he turned away from her she bit down hard
on her bottom lip, forgetting how tender it was.
The resultant pain made her cry out involuntarily,
causing him to stop and turn back to look at her.

The moment his glance focused on her swollen
lip her skin burned with hot embarrassment and
guilt.

'If I were you I should tell your boyfriend to be
a little less rough next time,' he told her contemptuously as he opened the front door.

He was halfway through the door when her
temper got the better of her, her voice husky with
anger as she told him shakily, 'I don't have a boyfriend, and for your information...' She stopped
abruptly, realising with shock what she had been
about to say.

'For my information what?' Gray prompted her.

He was looking at her mouth again. With a sick
surge of awareness Sarah realised just what she was
doing. She pressed her trembling lips together and
averted her head. Her whole body was shaking with
shock and panic, her eyes huge and dark with the
strain of her emotions.

Involuntarily her tongue-tip touched her swollen
lip, in a movement that was both explorative and
soothing; a gesture that betrayed to the man

watching her that she was completely unused to wearing such public evidence of a man's urgent desire.

Her lips were very soft and inviting, and now swollen and marked by that betraying bruise.

His body tightened warningly, the ache that had been with him when he had woken up intensifying sharply. It had been a long, long time since he had experienced such an almost uncontrollable surge of desire.

His sexual appetite had waned considerably during the last months of his marriage, and, unlike other men he knew, following his divorce he had not experienced any desire to go out and punish the rest of the female sex for his wife's infidelity and betrayal by entering into as many casual sexual relationships as he could.

It was true that there had been a couple of relationships, but both of them had initially been more cerebral than physical.

It came as a shock to him now to realise that he was capable of such a gut-deep physical, aching, compulsive need, and even worse that that need ... that ache should be directed at a woman whom he had determinedly and consciously held at a distance.

It was only later in his car, driving towards the factory, that he allowed himself to question why he should have felt that almost instantaneous awareness that she was someone against whom he would have to erect barricades; that she was someone who could threaten the emotional and physical control he exerted over his life.

He cursed himself, acknowledging that it had not been a good idea to employ her, but what alternative had he had? There was Robbie to consider. Robbie, who was his child...his son...Robbie, who, thanks to his mother's teachings, was afraid of him. And yet last night, frightened by his bad dream, Robbie had clung to him ... crying out to him, begging him to stay, and, holding the small and frighteningly fragile warmth of his small son in his arms, he had been overwhelmed by such a surge of love and pain ... love for the child who was, after all, a part of himself, and pain for all the years they had been apart, for all the trauma and sorrow that had marked their relationship.

He couldn't understand what was happening to him. After cutting himself off from his emotions, after telling himself that it was safer not to feel...not to love, he suddenly felt as though all his protection had been ripped away from him, leaving him raw and bleeding; leaving him vulnerable and in pain ... leaving him so confused and overwhelmed by his own feelings ... so shocked by the knowledge of what was happening to him ... He took a deep, steadying breath, shivering a little as he remembered how he had felt this morning looking at Sarah's swollen mouth; how he had been angrily, almost savagely jealous of the man who had the right to kiss her so passionately that she neither noticed nor cared that he was hurting her.

'I don't have a boyfriend,' she had said. And yet someone had touched her, kissed her. God, if he closed his eyes he could almost feel how it would be to have her mouth under his, to hear her soft cries of mingled pleasure and panic filling his ears, to touch the feminine curves of her throat, her breasts ... to feel her body beginning to respond to his and to know ...

He swore abruptly as the other driver sounded his horn at him and he realised that the lights had changed to green and that he had been sitting staring into space. This had got to stop. It was something there was no room for in his life ... something far too dangerous to allow into his life.

Once he had believed he was in love and that he was loved in return, and he had been wrong on both counts. He was never going to fall into that trap again. Never.

Never.

CHAPTER SEVEN

GRAY puzzled her, Sarah acknowledged. He was a man of such contradictions; a man who one moment could be the most caring and loving father to his child and yet who the next could withdraw from him almost as though he was afraid.

But afraid of what? Not, surely, of Robbie himself. Afraid of loving him, perhaps?

She frowned as she mulled the thought round in her head. It was almost two weeks since that fateful morning when she had arrived and found Gray sleeping in Robbie's bed, when he had in his sleep taken hold of her and caressed her and kissed her.

But no, she must not allow herself to think . . . to remember. She had always told herself more times than she cared to dwell upon that that incident was something around which she must build a fortification strong enough to ensure that its memory remained sealed away, untouched, undisturbed, unthought of for the rest of her life. Because if it wasn't . . . if she allowed it to dominate her thoughts and her feelings . . . She gave a deep shudder.

There was no future in the way she felt about Gray, no hope of his ever returning her feelings, of his ever coming to love her; she knew that from the way he treated her; from the cool civility that sometimes did not quite mask his antagonism towards her. He employed her as Robbie's nanny simply because he had not been able to find anyone else, but she knew now how much he resented her presence in his home, how much he resented her. She had seen the way he looked at her whenever Robbie ran to her for a cuddle, or whenever Robbie turned to her for something he wanted, and she knew that Gray disliked his son's growing emotional dependence on her.

She too was increasingly uneasy about it although, she suspected, for very different reasons. Robbie was a very vulnerable child. She had tried her best to widen his horizons, to introduce him to other children, and to some extent had been successful, but he still clung to her... still rushed quickly back to her side as though he was half afraid that she might have disappeared in his absence.

All quite a natural reaction, given the trauma he had been through, of course, but what Robbie needed in his life was someone permanent to whom he could give his love and his dependence, not someone like her who would only be a part of his life for a relatively short time.

It was true that Robbie was slowly becoming more responsive to his father, thanks to her own unceasing and gentle encouragement to him to see Gray as his friend rather than his enemy, and it was also true that Gray was becoming more responsive to him, showing a much gentler and more caring manner towards him than he had originally done, and yet sometimes, just as she was congratulating herself on having helped to forge a real bond between them, almost always—or so it seemed—when Gray was actually showing physical affection for Robbie he would draw back in some way from him, his body language clearly betraying his tension and wariness. Almost as though he was afraid of allowing himself to love his son. But what kind of man would feel like that? What kind of man would be afraid of loving his own child?

The kind who had once had that child taken from him and who perhaps in some illogical way feared that it might happen again? The kind who was afraid of allowing himself to love his child because, in his own deepest emotional awareness, love was so closely connected with pain that he could not differentiate between the two?

Sarah wished it was possible for her to talk more freely to Gray about his feelings and about her own fears that he was hurting Robbie with his rejection of him; that he was teaching Robbie to mistrust his own natural feelings, to reject his own natural desire to show his father love and affection; but, even if Gray had been more approachable, she doubted if she could have overcome the barrier of her own love for him enough to discuss the subject with the frankness it needed.

Because of that as much as because of her love for Gray she was beginning to seriously question if she was the right person to have charge of Robbie.

She had tried once, very hesitantly, to voice her doubts, but Gray had immediately grown grim-faced and taut-mouthed, accusing her of wanting to break the contract they had signed, and she had been forced to withdraw, knowing that it was impossible for her to voice all her disquiet in a way that would carry weight and conviction.

Gray mistrusted anything based on emotions, she had learned that much, and she reflected rather bitterly that he must once have loved Robbie's mother very much indeed to be so damaged by the destruction of their relationship.

And yet when she said as much at home to Sally, and Ross had overheard her, he had quickly shaken his head and told her, 'That's not what I've heard. By all accounts, the only reason they got married was because she was pregnant, and it seems he had to put pressure on her to go through with it. Apparently no one was really surprised when the marriage eventually failed, because it was common knowledge right from the start that whatever passion had led to Robbie's conception had turned to dead ashes long before their marriage, never mind his eventual birth.'

When Sarah made a soft sound of distress Ross shook his head again. 'You know your trouble, don't you?' he told her. 'You're far too soft-hearted... far too idealistic.'

'It's Robbie I feel sorry for,' Sally interrupted. 'Poor little boy. He's lucky he's got you, though, Sarah.'

Sarah shook her head. 'I'm afraid I could be doing more harm than good. He needs someone permanent in his life.'

'You mean you think Gray should remarry. Well, I doubt that he'll ever do that,' Ross told them. 'Rumour has it that he swore after the divorce that he'd never marry again, and he certainly doesn't come across as the kind of man it would be easy to get close to emotionally.'

'No, he isn't,' Sarah agreed feelingly.

And yet Gray wasn't a cold man. Even without that kiss she would have known that. Sometimes it was almost as though she could actually feel the

tension of everything that he was holding back
inside himself like a heat given off through his skin.

Since she had started working for him he seemed
to have become increasingly short-tempered with
her, increasingly critical and sometimes so unfairly
that she wondered if he was actually trying to
provoke her into breaking their contract and
leaving. And yet if he wanted to get rid of her he
only had to say so, surely, and he had not struck
her as the kind of man who would be too cowardly
to take that kind of action, using unfair manipu-
lation instead so that the burden of the decision lay
with her and not with him.

And yet there were times when he looked at her
almost as though he hated her.

He was also coming in later and later at night so
that she was forced to stay on well beyond her finishing time of six o'clock.

Whenever she mentioned this fact he countered
by reminding her that he had wanted her to live in.

Take tonight for instance, she reflected tiredly as
she ironed the last of Robbie's new school shirts.

Gray had promised that he would be back for
six, as she had explained to him that she was going
out for dinner, making up a foursome with Sally
and Ross and a business acquaintance of Ross's,
who was in the area for a couple of days on
business.

They were not trying to matchmake, Sally had
assured her when she had first mentioned the dinner
date; Sarah was not so sure, but she owed her cousin
far too much to refuse to go along with their plans.

However, it was now half-past seven, and she had
already had to ring Sally and warn her that it looked

as though she would not be able to join them, and
predictably and understandably her cousin had not
been too pleased.

'Oh, this really is the limit,' she had complained.
'It's almost as though he's done it deliberately. Have
you rung the factory?'

'Yes, and apparently no one seems to know where
he is. He left after lunch for a business appointment and said that he would be coming
straight home.' Sarah had bitten her lip and asked
her cousin anxiously, 'You don't think there's been
an accident, do you?'

Instantly Sally's anger had evaporated. 'Oh,
heavens, I hope not... but perhaps you'd better
check. Although I should have thought if something like that had happened... Still...'

'I'll ring the police,' Sarah had told her shakily.

Half an hour later, having confirmed as best she
could that there were no reports of Gray being involved in an accident, and yet shakily conscious of
the fact that that did not necessarily mean that
nothing had happened to him, she was just sitting
beside the phone when she heard the sound of his
car coming up the drive.

Instantly her fear turned to adrenalin-fuelled
rage, not just that he should be late, but that he
should have, even if unknowingly, put her through
so much anxiety and dread.

She was on her feet as he walked in through the
door, her face pale with strain, her eyes huge and
glittering in the darkness of the lamp-lit hallway, a
slim, almost ethereal silhouette whose feminine
shape and posture suddenly made Gray ache so un-

bearably and agonisingly that it took a physical
effort for him to stop himself from going up to her
and taking hold of her, from holding her and
touching her, from kissing her . . . not as though she
were a stranger, but as though she were a woman
with whom he had been so intimate already that
her body and its responses were so well known to
him, that her senses were so receptive to and so
aroused by him that he could make love to her there
where she stood, expunging all the irritations, the
pain, the anguish, the sheer weight of everything
that oppressed him by losing himself within her,
and that in doing so he would know that she under-
stood, that she accepted . . . that her feelings for
him . . . her love for him would allow him such a
selfish release of all that was pent up inside him,
without criticising or condemning him for it.

He had even taken the first step towards her when
suddenly his illusion was shattered, her voice cold
and ice-sharp as she demanded bitingly, 'You
promised me you would be back for six. I have a
dinner date tonight.'

The shock of that cold little voice, and the look
that accompanied it, was like a jet of iced water
touching too hot skin, causing an almost physical
pain within him, so that he retaliated immediately,
for once his emotional guard failing him as he threw
back at her, 'What stopped you leaving, then, if
your dinner date was so damned important?'

Sarah stared at him in shocked anger.

'You know that I can't leave Robbie on his own,'
she told him.

'Why not?' Gray demanded savagely. 'His
mother did. In fact, it was because she left him on

his own so much that her own mother eventually intervened and took charge of him. Well, if your damned dinner date is so important to you . . . more important than Robbie . . . don't let me keep you. In fact, if it's so damned important to you you can leave now, and don't bother coming back.'

His attack was so unexpected, so flagrantly unfair that Sarah could only stare at him in shocked disbelief.

She could feel the tears starting to sting her eyes, and knew with appalling clarity that if she stayed where she was she would be unable to stop herself from bursting into tears. The last thing she could cope with now was to have Gray witness her emotional weakness and vulnerability, and so she did the only thing she was capable of doing: she snatched up her bag and, averting her face, she almost ran past Gray and through the still half-open door.

Crashing the gears of her car in her frantic desire to get away, she drove down the drive, stopping just before she got to the main road so that she could steady her nerves and blow her nose.

It made no difference to the tears now flooding her eyes, she discovered as she gulped back the sobs threatening to overwhelm her.

It was just shock, she told herself. Just shock, that was all. But beneath her shock ran a quickly rising tide of misery and pain. It made no difference telling herself that she had known all along what Gray was like; that she had warned herself not to allow her feelings for him to paint him in softer, warmer colours than the harsh, critical shades which really portrayed him . . . that it was her

own fault if now she was suffering for that
vulnerability.

But to attack her like that when he was the one...
She gulped back her tears and blew her nose again.

She still could not believe that he had actually
dismissed her. That he had actually lost his temper
with such savagery and immediacy... that he had
actually lost emotional control like that when he
was always... always so strongly in control of what
he felt and how he reacted... when he hardly ever
said a single word that had not been pre-
judged... when he never made a move that wasn't
guarded and wary.

By the time she reached the cottage her temper
had cooled, leaving her feeling sick and shaky.

She had never been a violently emotional person,
always thinking of herself as a little too quiet, her
emotions contained and controlled, but this
evening...

She gave a small shudder as she let herself into
the empty cottage and filled the kettle with water
to make herself a drink.

Perhaps because of the too abrupt swing from
the fear of thinking that Gray might actually be
injured, and lying helpless and unaware in some
distant hospital, to the bitter reality of his arrival
home whole and unhurt, and so patently uncaring
of the anxiety, the fear he had caused her, never
mind the fact that he was so late when he had
known that she was going out, had been the cause
of her unexpectedly intense anger.

Yes, she had some cause for reacting the way she
had, but as for Gray himself... he had seemed
almost to welcome her anger... to invite and incite

it, and yet he must have known that he was in the
wrong. And then, to have dismissed her...

She gave another shudder, deeper this time. She
would have to go back, of course, if only to explain
to Robbie. But how could she explain...what would
she say? She certainly didn't want to do anything
that might prejudice the very fragile relationship
Robbie was trying to establish with his father.

Another different kind of anger swept over her.
How could Gray be so selfish, so uncaring of
Robbie's feelings? Didn't he realise how this could
affect the little boy?

It was late when Sally and Ross returned, and of
course they had to hear the whole story, Ross
frowning when she related Gray's reaction to her
own anger.

'It seems to me that it's a situation you're well
out of,' he announced when he had heard her out.

'But Robbie——' Sarah began.

Ross shook his head. 'I know how concerned you
are for him, Sarah,' he told her. 'As I said before,
you're far too soft-hearted. But, to some extent,
while you're living here with us we *are* responsible
for you. Yes, I know you're an adult...and fully
capable of making your own decisions, but I'm not
at all happy with the way Gray has started behaving
towards you. In fact I'm half tempted to go round
there and have a word with him...'

'Oh, no...*please* don't do that,' Sarah begged
him.

She had gone so white and looked so strained
that, even though he was still frowning and looking
very grave, Ross gave in and said, 'All right, if you
prefer me not to, but I can't pretend that I'm not

relieved that you won't be working for him any
longer.'

'I'll have to go back to see Robbie,' Sarah told
them both. 'I can't just leave him, even if Gray
does explain to him.'

'Why don't you leave it until either Sally or I are
able to go with you?' Ross suggested, but Sarah
immediately shook her head.

'No, I'm not hiding behind either of you. As you
said, I'm an adult and as such I am fully capable
of fighting my own battles. Tonight I was off
guard . . . but tomorrow . . .'

She was awake well before dawn, hardly having
slept at all, and she dressed carefully, not in her
normal work clothes, but in a smart sober suit that
reflected the sternness of her mood. She had no
intention of trying to persuade Gray to change his
mind, of grovelling at his feet, so to speak, and
begging for her job back, but she was determined
that she was going to see Robbie and that she was
going to explain to him as gently and as best she
could what had happened, without in any way
laying any blame at his father's door. For Robbie's
sake, she could not . . . would not do that.

When she drew up outside the house half an hour
later it was ablaze with lights. Even before she was
out of the car the front door was flung open and
Gray came racing down the steps towards her,
asking her urgently as she opened the car door,
'Robbie . . . is he with you?'

Robbie with *her*? In his anxiety Gray had taken
hold of her arm. He was standing so close to her
that she could smell the hot, sharp scent of maleness

and fear that clung to him. An overnight growth
of beard darkened his jaw. He was wearing a T-
shirt and a worn pair of jeans; he looked, she recognised, as though he had been up half the night,
and the anxiety that surrounded him almost like an
aura was now enveloping her as well, her eyes
darkening with fear as she demanded sharply, 'No,
Robbie isn't with me. Why?'

'I can't find him. I brought some work home with
me last night. I don't know why...but I couldn't
sleep well.' He was avoiding looking at her, Sarah
noticed, his voice uneven and harsh as though it
masked emotions he was reluctant to betray.

'I was up early. I went to look in on Robbie and
he wasn't there. I've checked the house but there
doesn't seem to be any sign of him.'

A shocked feeling of disbelief was gripping Sarah.

'Last night,' she asked him sharply. 'Did you go
up to see him last night after I'd left?'

Now he focused on her, his eyes bloodshot and
vague with emotional strain.

He hesitated and then shook his head...and even
though she had not voiced her criticism he defended himself bleakly.

'I'd brought some work home with me. I thought
he would be asleep. I didn't want to disturb him.'

You mean *you* didn't want to be bothered, Sarah
thought bleakly, but she kept the thought to herself.
She could tell from his expression just how much
he was suffering...just how guilty he felt. Nothing
could be achieved by criticising him now.

When she remained silent there was a small
pause, and then to her surprise he said gruffly,
'Thanks.'

The shock of it made her look at him, her eyes
wide and unguarded as they betrayed her emotions.

'For what?' she asked him shakily.

'For not saying what I know you must be
thinking. That I should have gone up to check on
him.' The emotion . . . the despair . . . the guilt in his
voice made her body physically ache in sympathy
with him. 'God knows, I know I should have done
it . . . but I didn't, and now he's gone.'

'You're sure he's actually left the house?' Sarah
asked him.

'As sure as I can be. I've searched every room
and cupboard twice over. My one hope was that he
might have come to you.'

Her mouth had gone dry with fear and anxiety.

'The police,' she asked him quietly. 'Have
you . . .?'

He shook his head.

'No. I was just about to ring you, to find out if
he was with you, and if not to ask for your advice.'

He had been going to ask *her* for advice. The
shock of it made her gape up at him.

'You don't believe me? I'm not surprised. After
the way I behaved last night . . . Oh, God . . . where
on earth is he? Why has he left? I thought he was
settling down . . . coming to realise . . .'

'I think we'd better ring the police,' Sarah told
him gently. Without realising what she was doing
she had reached out and touched his arm; a
soothing, comforting gesture, an automatic response to his anguish, and yet when he stopped
speaking, and looked first at where her hand rested
on his arm and then at her, she suddenly became
heart-jerkingly aware of the hard heat of his skin,

of its fine covering of silky hair, of the way his muscles tensed beneath her touch, of the sheer living, breathing maleness of him.

Her breath caught in her throat, she couldn't breathe...couldn't think...couldn't move, and then suddenly she jerked back from him, her face paling with awareness and guilt.

How could she be feeling like this when all her thoughts, all her emotions ought to be concentrated on Robbie? How *could* she have ever allowed herself to feel that searching shocking surge of physical desire, especially when Gray himself had made it so clear how little he liked her, never mind how little he desired her?

She rang the police, dialling the number with shaky fingers. Their response was instant and somehow comforting. There would be someone with them within half an hour, they assured her, and in the meantime they must try not to panic.

Try not to panic? How was that possible? She only had to think of the way she had first met Robbie...of his naïve belief then that he could make his own way to London.

Her heart almost stopped. She turned to Gray.

'You don't think he's heading for London, do you...for his grandmother's housekeeper? When I first met him...'

Gray shook his head. 'I've no idea. You know more about him...the way he thinks, the way he's likely to act, than I do. I was so sure he'd go to you. That was all I could think of—that he'd be with you. God help me. I even thought that you had...' He stopped shaking his head, but she had already guessed what he had been about to say.

'You honestly thought that? That I would encourage him to leave home . . . a child of that age?'
Although she tried to remain calm, her voice betrayed her.

'I'm sorry . . . I . . . I just don't seem to be able to
think straight these days. As you've probably heard
on the grapevine, my experience of your sex hasn't
been entirely conducive to . . . to trust.'

Sarah looked gravely at him.

'Trust, like any other emotion, is a two-way
thing,' she told him quietly. 'I would never do anything that might hurt Robbie, no matter what my
personal feelings towards you might be. I know I
over-reacted last night.' This seemed as good a time
as any to say what had to be said, now that the
barriers were momentarily down between them and
they were joined together in their anxiety for
Robbie. 'But I felt so guilty about letting my cousin
and her husband down at the last minute, especially when they were entertaining a business
client.'

Gray was frowning. 'You were having dinner with
your cousin?'

'I was making a foursome with them,' Sarah told
him. She broke off as she heard a car coming up
the drive. 'That must be the police.'

'Yes,' Gray agreed tersely, heading for the front
door. 'I'll go and let them in.'

Half an hour later, having gone through his
wardrobe and cupboards, Sarah had managed to
give the police a detailed list of what Robbie was
wearing.

His decision to leave had probably been made on
impulse, the WPC told her, trying to comfort her,

because it was their experience that when children
of no matter what age planned to leave home they
invariably took some favourite possession and a
change of clothes with them. Robbie had taken
nothing, and, to judge from the state of his drawers,
he had dressed himself in something of a hurry as
well.

'Did anything happen yesterday... anything at
all which might have caused him to be upset?'

Sarah thought and then shook her head. 'Not as
far as I know.'

'A quarrel with another child... or even with
you?' the grave-eyed WPC pressed her.

Again Sarah shook her head, slowly going
through the events of the previous day.

She had already given the other woman a brief
description of Robbie's past and how she had come
to be looking after him, without saying anything
to suggest that Robbie's relationship with Gray was
in any way unsatisfactory. If Gray chose to tell them
otherwise that was his decision, and it was not one
which she intended to make for him.

They were interviewed separately and then
together; searching questions were asked about
Robbie and his background, questions that made
Sarah wince, although she noticed that Gray
answered them all honestly and quietly, even when
the answers did not reflect entirely well on him.

Once or twice the sergeant interviewing him
paused, allowing him more time to respond, and
once, when Gray admitted that he had not checked
on Robbie during the evening, he said sympathetically, 'Try not to blame yourself, sir. It's something
we're all guilty of doing at times.'

Sarah was asked separately and away from Gray if she felt that Robbie was in any way either physically or emotionally maltreated by his father. Quickly she shook her head, knowing thankfully that it was the truth. Gray might not be an ideal father, but she acquitted him of wanting to hurt Robbie in any way.

When the police had gathered as much information as they could they left, having offered to leave someone with them, an offer which Gray refused.

Once they had gone Sarah suggested diffidently that she too should leave, thinking that he must want to be on his own, but to her surprise he shook his head, saying quickly, pleadingly almost, 'No, please...if you could stay...'

When she made no response he added hesitantly, as though he was groping for unfamiliar words and motions, 'You know Robbie. He knows you...needs you...loves you. If...when they do find him...if you are here...'

So it was for Robbie's sake that he wanted her to stay and not his own, but then, what had she expected?

She had rung Sally, of course, to let her know what was happening, and immediately her cousin had agreed that she must stay.

Halfway through the interminable morning when she went upstairs to Robbie's room, needing the comfort of being among his things, she found that Gray was already there, sitting on his son's bed, with his back to her, his head bowed as he held Robbie's favourite bear.

She was just about to back silently out of the room, when he said roughly, 'No, don't go. God, when I think of how little he is...how vulnerable...I should be out looking for him...not sitting here, waiting.'

Sarah shook her head, and then, realising that he couldn't see her, went up to him and told him huskily, 'No, the police said we were to stay here...in case there was any news.'

'I feel so helpless,' Gray protested. 'I feel I should be doing something. He's *my* son, for God's sake...my child.' He paused, and then said in a much harsher voice, 'I suppose you think this is all my fault, but, believe me, you can't blame me more than I blame myself. If only I had checked up on him.'

As she had done before, Sarah reached out instinctively to touch him, a simple, silent gesture of comfort and compassion, her throat too taut with fear for her to be able to speak, but then Gray turned round, his movements blind and uncoordinated, a look of savage self-contempt on his face as he cried out to her, 'Why...why has he done it? Is he really so afraid of me...does he really hate me so much?'

Immediately Sarah shook her head. 'No, no, of course he doesn't,' she told him softly.

Somehow she must have moved closer to him because when she looked down on his own bent head there were only inches between them, and, although part of her warned her that it was the last thing she ought to do, the compassion and caring that was so deeply ingrained in her personality motivated her now, moving her to reach out and place her hand against his head, a silent gesture of comfort and sympathy.

'Oh, God, Sarah, if anything happens to him...'

But that wasn't why her whole body suddenly went rigid with shock...as his action over-set everything she thought she knew about him, Gray moved awkwardly, putting his arms around her, holding her so tightly that she could hardly get her breath, his head pillowed heavily against her breasts as the tortured words were torn from him.

'Gray...' Her voice trembled unconsciously, pleading with him to do what she could not do herself, but when he didn't move, but simply seemed to tighten his grip on her, his body starting to shake as his emotions engulfed him, Sarah knew that it had to be she who broke this unexpected physical contact between them.

CHAPTER EIGHT

SARAH reached out to break the physical contact between them, but, as though Gray sensed what she was about to do, without raising his head, the words muffled against her body, his breath a hot, vital force that penetrated the thin fabric of her blouse to make her sensitive flesh urgently and erotically aware of him, he begged her hoarsely, 'No, please, Sarah. Just let me...just hold me.'

And then, as she stood there, her body trembling with the shocked awareness of her own response to him, he swore suddenly and savagely, telling her, 'Oh, God, I don't know what's happening to me any more. You're on my mind night and day, do you know that? I dream about you...wake up aching for you...imagining...God, I need you so much now. I...'

He tensed suddenly, as though abruptly becoming aware of what he was saying, of her shock...and then he started to lift his head away from her body, his face averted from her as he added, his voice raw with self-disgust, 'Even now, when all I should be thinking about is Robbie, I still want you...still——'

'It's the shock,' Sarah told him wildly. 'It sometimes has an odd effect on people. It makes them behave irrationally. It...'

She stopped speaking as she looked down and saw that a couple of the buttons on her shirt had pulled free of the buttonholes, leaving her creamy cleavage fully exposed.

Her hand trembled as she reached for the button, her panicky movement catching Gray's attention. Her whole body tensed as she realised he was looking at her, her breath quickening, her chest rising and falling far too quickly, betraying her agitation.

As though it had received an inaudible but positive command from him, the hand she had raised to cover her bare flesh in an instinctive gesture of feminine modesty fell away, and, while her pulse and heart-rate increased frantically in response to their sensual awareness of Gray's physical desire, all her other physical responses were slowed down almost to the point of paralysis, a hazy, dreamy, almost hypnotic, drugged state of inertia full of brilliant colours and sensitised by her growing feminine awareness of the fact that Gray wanted her, that he needed her, that he desired her.

All her ability to reason or question was suspended, obliterated by the greater power of her emotional and physical knowledge that for once the barriers between them were down; that for once they were meeting on equal ground; that for once Gray was casting aside the armour plating of his dislike of her and allowing her to see the real vulnerable human being behind that armour.

For once they were united instead of on opposing sides, sharing their anxiety for Robbie's safety, and because it was her nature to do so, because her instinctive response to any fellow human in intense pain was to offer them comfort and succour, Sarah had no thought of repulsing Gray, no thought of withdrawing herself from him, of denying him.

What she hadn't bargained for, though, was that her own need...her own desire, should be as sharply pitched, as shockingly intense, as his.

She knew that she loved and desired him, but, for her, sexual desire, even when heightened by the intensity of the love she felt for him, had been something that was softened and mellowed by an instinctive reticence, a shyness almost, coupled with a lack of anything more than the kind of experience gained from youthful experimentation.

And yet now suddenly, as Gray held her, groaning her name against the soft, smooth flesh of her breasts, tugging the rest of the blouse buttons free of the buttonholes, she was overcome by an almost savage flare of corresponding desire, a need so intense that it stopped the breath in her throat and made her long to cry out with impatience, to wrench her own clothes from her body and then his, to lie with him flesh to flesh. Her whole body went rigid with the intensity of what she was feeling. She had to bite down hard on her bottom lip to stop herself from urging him to hurry... She could feel his hands trembling as he tugged off her blouse; she could smell the sharply acrid male scent of his skin with its heat and muskiness and suddenly realised that the reason for this was that without even knowing she was doing so she had started to wrench his T-shirt free of his jeans, her hands splaying possessively against his body, and shockingly all the realisation of what she was doing did was to reinforce and increase the heat burning inside her so that she

heard herself moan in sharp frustrated protest at
not being able to remove his T-shirt completely.

Against her body Gray tensed. The heat of his
breath against her skin made her tremble and ache
with a wanton need to be completely free of her
clothes so that not just his hands but his mouth as
well could ease the torment of need escalating so
rapidly inside her.

'What is it?' she heard him asking her, and then,
as though the tension in her body answered his
question for him, he demanded more roughly, as
he released her to strip off his T-shirt, 'Is it this,
Sarah? Is it this that you want...my flesh against
yours...my body next to yours?'

She was trembling so violently that speech was
impossible, but the way her body was reacting to
the sight of him, to the words he was saying to her,
to the heat and scent of his flesh, was a far more
betraying response than any verbal answer she could
have given him.

In a gesture totally unfamiliar to her, something
she would never normally have done or imagined
herself doing, she closed her eyes, swaying closer
to him, unconsciously heightening the allure of her
own body, her breasts covered only by the fine lace
of her bra where he had pushed open her shirt,
reaching for him, smoothing her hands over his skin
with eager, aching intensity, her fingers trembling
as she touched him, unaware of just how sensual
and arousing her response to him was until he cried
out her name in a harshly guttural voice and
gathered her to him, his mouth hot and moist as
he caressed the taut line of her throat, his hands
cupping her breasts, a little hesitantly at first, as

though he was half afraid of hurting or frightening her. But then, when she pushed closer to him, wordlessly pleading with him, he reached behind her to unfasten her bra, his hands moulding her naked breasts, the sensation of the male roughness of his skin against her own tender softness so erotically stimulating that she cried out in sharp need, her hands tensing into the warm flesh of his shoulders, a tiny whimper of stifled pleasure heightening the aroused tension of their breathing when he touched her erect nipples.

She heard him say something, and thought at first that the intensity of her response must have shocked him, but even as she was tensing, trying to control the way her body ached for him, he was pushing her down against the bed, pinning the lower half of her body beneath his own so that she was immediately and exultantly conscious of his arousal, shockingly excited by the weight and the heat of him between her thighs while his mouth dragged feverishly along her throat and then lower to where his hands were cupping her breasts.

As though he knew exactly what she was feeling, as though he shared the compulsive, almost violent surge of desire that held her in thrall, he made no attempt at gentle exploration of her swollen breasts, instead his mouth fiercely drawing on the aching hardness of her nipple. The sensation that shot through her made her back arch as her whole body went into a violent spasm of pleasure, a taut, haunting cry escaping her lips, her hands clutching at his arms, his shoulders, his back, as her body became one unbearable ache of anguished need.

She had never known there could be a sensation like this, a need like this, a desire so intense that it obliterated everything else, that it reduced the entire universe to that one point on her body, where his mouth caused her such a sensation of pleasure that it was almost unendurable.

He was saying something to her, words that flowed over her with the balm of the soft drag of his mouth against her skin as he tried to soothe the intensity of her desire. He was telling her that she was so exquisitely sensitive that she was making him lose his self-control; that his desire for her was threatening to overwhelm him; that he wanted her more than he wanted life itself, Sarah recognised as she tried half incoherently to respond to his husky disjointed words, and to tell him that she felt the same way; that she ached inside so much for him that unless he soothed that ache with the hard pulse of his body the agony of it would kill her.

She felt him unfastening her skirt, guiding her hands to the fastening of his jeans and then, as though unable to bear any kind of delay, taking over the task himself, ripping off his jeans with savage unsteadiness, while she looked with totally uninhibited and unfamiliar avid intensity at his body.

He was everything that a man should have been and her heartbeat increased to a frantic race of rapidity as she stared at him, aching for him, loving him, her senses bemused by the compulsion that drove her.

She hadn't forgotten about Robbie. He was still there, a different kind of ache, a different kind of pain, her anguish for him somehow or other the

motivating force that had kindled this unexpected
and uninhibited passion. It was as though somehow
being with Gray like this was some kind of
ritual... some kind of primitive appeasement of a
hungry and cruel power... some kind of ritual sac-
rifice of self, that made her shake with shocked reaction to her own lack of control at the very same
time as she revelled in the way that, having stripped
off his own clothes, Gray removed the rest of hers,
and then simply looked at her.

Up until now her body had been her own private
territory, something she fed and clothed and kept
reasonably fit, but not particularly something that
she thought of as sensual or erotic in any way, and
yet now...

Was she imagining it, or did her skin have a new
gleam, a new softness... had her body always
known how to abandon itself into such feminine
wantonness... how to curve and move so that it
would make a man shudder and then groan before
reaching out to drag one trembling hand along its
supine curve... a hand that tightened almost possessively against her waist and then lingered on the
round warmth of her thigh so that she moved instinctively and incitingly against its pressure, inviting its possession of the hidden feminine core of
her body?

And all the time he watched her, his eyes registering every tiny response and reflecting it back to
her so that her own desire was heightened by his,
so that, long before she was crying out to him that
she wanted more than the erotic caress of his fingers
against her intimate flesh, he had read her desire
to have his body within her own in the sudden

shocked perception that had darkened her eyes, and
was responding to it.

It had been a long time since she had first made
love, the fumbling and unsatisfactory consum-
mation of a teenage passion which had left her
feeling cheated and wondering what all the excitement was actually about, and, as though he had
somehow sensed this, he hesitated, as if afraid to
hurt her, but Sarah had a woman's knowledge of
her own body, and of its needs and its capabilities,
and she arched up against him, holding him to her,
feeling his body tremble as he was unable to hold
back on his response to her.

It was an intense, almost savage-edged coming
together, a frantic explosion of a mutual need to
expiate their anguish and fear, their desire escalating with violent speed to a point of fierce explosion which left Sarah so weak that she was
incapable of moving, every muscle turned to jelly,
the hot, slow tears of sexual release seeping from
her eyes.

Unable to raise her hand to rub them away, she
let them fall. Gray had started to move away from
her, but now he stopped, his fingers gentle as he
brushed away her tears, his mouth tender as he
licked the moisture from her skin.

The unexpectedness of such tenderness after the
compulsive violence of their coming together
brought a huge lump of pain to her throat. While
she had been held in thrall to the intensity of their
mutual need there had been no ability within her
to think of anything other than the immediacy of
the moment, but now that moment was over, and
she was coming back down to earth, to the sick

realisation of what she had done... She wanted to
move, to cover herself, to crawl away somewhere
and preferably die there, she realised in sick shame,
but she felt too exhausted, too drained to move,
and, besides, Gray was still holding her.

She closed her eyes, wanting, as she had not done
before, to conceal her expression and her vulnerability from him.

She had no need to ask herself what had motivated *him*. It had been sex, that was all, a physical
outlet for his anxiety over Robbie. It wasn't such
an unusual male reaction to that kind of nightmare
situation, after all... rather like a divorcing couple
who suddenly discovered a need within themselves,
just as their emotional commitment to one another
was over, to indulge in fiercely physical sex, sometimes when sex of any kind had long ago faded
almost entirely from their relationship... but then
she realised that Gray was still holding her, still
touching her, and she started to tremble, her
thoughts becoming confused and disjointed. He was
kissing her, slowly tracing the bone-structure of her
face, his thumb-tip caressing the soft outline of her
mouth, while his tongue explored the delicate con-
tours of her ear, sending convulsive shivers of
pleasure racing over her skin, re-arousing her body
in a way that five minutes ago she would have sworn
was impossible.

This time there was a deliberate, almost controlled slowness about the way that Gray touched
her, a desire that, although equally intense, was
somehow less compulsive, less driven, so that,
where before she had experienced a hard, sharp-
edged sexual hunger, this time she seemed to be

wrapped up in a softening languor of sensuality that made her feel as if she was slowly drifting deeper and deeper into an erotic cocoon of mindless bliss. A sensation that was heightened by the slow scalding heat that poured through her body when Gray caressed every inch of her skin with the delicately intimate exploration of his mouth, taking her response to him to such a pitch that she cried out against the slow inexorable pressure of it, wanting both the release of fulfilment and yet at the same time the heightened pleasure of prolonging her slowly spiralling desire.

The seductive caress of his mouth against her inner thigh; the intimate stroke of his tongue against the most sensitive and delicate part of her body— these were things that frayed the fragile cord of her self-control to the point where it finally snapped under the pressure, causing her to cry out to Gray how much she needed him; how much she wanted him; how much she ached for him, and to have that needing, that wanting, that aching appeased by the tormentingly erotic thrust of his body as it moved powerfully and purposefully within her own, so that her flesh responded to his in fluidly rhythmic counterpoint that made him gasp out her name in the final fiercely compulsive seconds of physical intensity before the climax came.

Later, drifting into an exhausted sleep she couldn't fight off, Sarah was aware of Gray moving away from her and of trying to stop him, of wanting to beg him to stay with her but of being too tired to form the words.

It was the phone that woke her, bringing her sharply awake, Robbie's name on her lips as she

sat up in bed, wincing as her body revealed its
physical lassitude. It was only her total nudity that
stopped her from running downstairs, in her anxiety
to find out if there was any news of Robbie, forcing
her to stop long enough to pull on her clothes, ignoring her heightened feminine awareness of the
sensual aura that clung to her skin. There would
be time later to shower and change; right now her
one concern was Robbie; a concern that was fast
becoming fuelled by a deep-seated guilt that she
could ever have allowed herself to abandon herself
to the kind of physical sexuality she had shared with
Gray, especially at such a time. It made no difference telling herself that people often reacted
strangely under intense pressure; that might be
Gray's explanation for his behaviour, but she was
not going to allow herself that kind of self-
deception. She loved Gray... and she had wanted
him, but she had never dreamed she would ever
behave in such an abandoned and ill-considered
fashion, especially when she knew that Gray felt
nothing for her.

As she pulled on her clothes her body chose
traitorously to remind her that, if nothing else, Gray
had most definitely wanted her physically.

She froze where she was, aching with self-disgust.
Had wanted *her*, or had simply wanted the release
of having sex with someone... *anyone*.

Sickness clawed at her stomach. Why hadn't she
thought of that before... told herself that
before... not waited until now, when it was too
late... when she had well and truly made a complete fool of herself, abandoning her principles, her
beliefs, behaving like a... like... like a wanton to

whom sex was an appetite that was only physical, rather than, as she truly believed, only being of any real worth when it was married to emotional and mental bonding with one's partner?

Well, what bonding was there between her and Gray? None...none at all.

Apart from the fact that they both loved Robbie...that they were both desperately concerned for him...that they had both been torn away from their normal modes of behaviour by the unbearable intensity of their anguish; and their inability to do a single thing to help him; their helplessness in the face of that anguish.

What was she doing? Looking for excuses for the inexcusable. She gave a deep shudder. What had happened was something she could understand and accept happening between an established couple— say, the parents of a missing child, who, driven by their need to seek comfort in one another, might become so sexually and intensely aware of one another that their feelings could result in that kind of heightened intensity...but for two people who were not lovers...two people, one of whom openly disliked the other...two people, one of whom secretly loved the other...

The sharp ping of the telephone receiver being replaced focused her thoughts back on Robbie. She was dressed now, and she hurried along the landing to find Gray standing in the hallway. He looked up as she ran downstairs and then looked away from her, almost as though he couldn't bear the sight of her. She froze where she was, fighting a cowardly longing to burst into tears and crawl away, but then she reminded herself that he was as much to blame

for what had happened between them as she had
been, and held her head up proudly, asking him
tightly, 'The phone... Was there any news of
Robbie?'

He shook his head, still refusing to look at her.

'No. Not yet. That was just the police checking
to see if he'd turned up. Apparently they've checked
and he hasn't been seen anywhere, which would
suggest that he might be trying to head for London.
Oh, God, when I think how young he is. How vulnerable. If only...'

Abruptly he turned his head and looked at her,
the shock of being subjected to such a piercing gaze
sending a wash of hot colour flooding her skin.

'About what happened... before... I... I don't
know what to say... other than to——'

'You don't need to say anything,' Sarah interrupted him desperately. He was going to tell her
that it should never have happened; that he had
never intended it to happen. If he had written it in
the sky in ten-foot letters for the whole world to
see he couldn't have made it more plain that he
wanted her to know that he did not really want
her... that he did not really feel anything for her.

'We both acted out of character.' She stumbled
over the words, refusing to give in to her pain and
anguish. She wasn't going to let him think that she
had no pride. She wasn't going to let him stand
there and be the one to say that what had happened
meant nothing. Even if it *was* a lie, she was going
to make sure that he believed she was as equally
anxious as him to deny the whole incident. 'I... I
believe people do sometimes behave in ways that
are... out of character under intense pressure.

It's . . . it's best that we both forget the whole thing. After all, once Robbie is found . . . well, there won't be any need for us to have any further contact, will there?'

'No, I don't suppose there will,' Gray agreed in an oddly rough voice. 'Unless, of course . . .' He broke off, still focusing on her, waiting almost pointedly for her to say something, she realised, although exactly what it was he was expecting her to say she didn't know until he added curtly, 'If there should be any . . . any consequences . . . then of course I'd want to know . . . to . . . to take responsibility.'

Any consequences? Sarah's eyes widened in shock as she realised what he meant. The last thing she had considered when they had made love was that she might become pregnant, but now suddenly she went cold and sick as the reality of that possibility hit her. The shock of it was so intense that she had to clutch hold of the banister to quell the nausea rising up inside her.

Pregnant . . . but no . . . she couldn't be. Not so quickly . . . not like that, without any fore-thought . . . any planning. What was the matter with her? she derided herself. Was she so stupid that she didn't really know just how little it took to become pregnant? Just how easily it could happen? An 'accident' was how most women euphemistically described that kind of conception. A happy accident, perhaps, for most of them, but for her . . .

Inside her something shrivelled and died as she acknowledged how much in other circumstances she would have wanted Gray's child . . . how very special it would feel to know that that child had been con-

ceived at such a time of trauma ... how very special
that child would always be ... but only if it had been
conceived in mutual love ... only if Gray had felt
about her the way she felt about him ... only if he
had loved her ... needed her ... wanted her for
succour and love. Which he most certainly had not.

The pain inside her was so intense, so unbearable
that it made her lash out against him with
uncharacteristic cruelty to say sharply, 'Well, let's
hope there won't be. After all, you never really
wanted Robbie, did you, and——?'

'That's not true.' His face went tense and set.
'Oh, I know it's what both you and Robbie think,
and possibly everyone else as well, but it simply
isn't true.' He gave a harsh laugh. 'My God, Robbie
would never even have been born if the decision
had been left to his mother. She wanted to get rid
of him. I had to blackmail her financially into going
through with the pregnancy.

'It's ironic; without the money I promised her
plus my agreement to a divorce, she'd have had
Robbie aborted, and yet once he was born, once
she realised what a powerful and permanent hold
having him gave her over me, she refused to go
through with our previous agreement that she would
hand Robbie over to me. She never wanted to con-
ceive my child, or any child, and I refuse to believe
that she ever truly loved Robbie. She didn't even
have him living with her. It was her mother who
brought Robbie up.'

The bitterness in his voice made Sarah shiver, her
own anguish forgotten as she heard the unmis-
takable ring of truth in his voice.

'But you sound as though you hate her.' She gave another shudder, the words an instinctive response to all the pain she could see so clearly in his eyes. 'And yet you must have loved her...you must both have loved one another once.'

'Must we?' His mouth twisted bitterly. 'We certainly desired one another, but, as we both quickly discovered, lust is no substitute for love, and by the time we'd made that discovery it was too late. Robbie was on the way and we were married. Oh, God, where is he?'

The anguish in his voice made her start to move instinctively towards him, wanting to offer him comfort, to share his pain, but then she stopped abruptly, remembering what had happened between them and the fact that she was the last person he would want any kind of comfort from.

She ached to be able to do something...anything other than simply having to wait passively here, letting others do the searching...the work, and, if she found the waiting onerous, then how much more so must Gray, who was, after all, not the kind of man used to being anything other than in complete command?

When, half an hour later, the phone rang again both of them froze, simply staring at it, neither of them apparently able to make a move, until suddenly Gray lunged towards it, grabbing the receiver, saying his name tersely.

In the silence that followed, while he listened to whoever was on the other end of the line, Sarah's stomach muscles knotted with tension and fear.

It seemed to be a lifetime before she heard him saying dully, 'Yes. Yes, I understand. Thank you.'

And then he was replacing the receiver, with a slow deliberate care that made her start to tremble with nervous dread. When he turned towards her his face was completely expressionless, his eyes vacant and dull.

Her heart seemed to plummet downwards, like a lift gone out of control, her lips so dry that she had to wet them before asking in a raw, cracked voice, 'Robbie? Have they...?'

'They've found him.'

His voice seemed to echo inside her skull, as a huge wave of sick pain engulfed her. He sounded so drained, so shocked... so...

She started to sway slightly, her shock registering in her face.

As he turned to her and saw her Gray made a sudden harsh exclamation beneath his breath, and then the next moment he was coming towards her, gripping the tops of her arms, telling her fiercely, 'Sarah, it's all right. Robbie's all right. He's safe and completely unharmed... They found him in a ramshackle old hut where he'd taken refuge. It's just... it's just that he's told the police that he doesn't want to come home. They've asked me to go down to the station. I was wondering... I know it's an imposition after everything that's happened... but... would you come with me?'

Sarah couldn't speak. All she could do was nod her head, still unable to truly take in the fact that Robbie was well and safe, after believing that he was not.

Gray drove them down to the police station. Outwardly he was in control of himself and his emotions, but Sarah was learning to look beneath

the surface, and she could tell that inwardly he was
suffering almost as much as she was herself.

How could she ever have been so cruel as to
suggest that he hadn't wanted Robbie, when she
had guessed all along how much the little boy meant
to him, even if he had refused to show it? She was
shocked by her own capacity for inflicting pain on
him, even if it had been done in a desperate attempt to defend and protect herself.

If she should have conceived his child the last
thing she would ever consider doing would be
aborting it. But then, all women were not the same,
and, from what Robbie had innocently told her
about his mother, Sarah had already formed the
opinion that the other woman had been vain and
shallow, far more interested in herself and fulfilling
her own wants and desires than in her child. She
had been manipulative as well, using Robbie as a
pawn against his father and then cruelly putting into
Robbie's head the belief that his father was someone
to fear.

When they reached the station they were ushered
straight into a small room, where a very tired and
frightened Robbie was being comforted by a WPC.
The moment he saw Sarah he broke free of the other
woman and came hurtling towards her. Instinctively she bent down so that they were on the same
level, cradling him to her, while she stroked his hair,
and felt her eyes burn with tears at the relief of
holding his wiry little boy's body against her own.

On the other side of the room Gray was talking
to the detective who had led the hunt for Robbie.
They were keeping their voices low, but Sarah
caught the odd word.

The detective was saying something about 'a quarrel' and Robbie being 'upset', but Robbie was crying so hard that she couldn't make out any more.

It was only much later, when Robbie had been put to bed and was safely fast asleep and she finally could bring herself to leave Robbie's room, that she learned the full story from Gray, who was waiting for her downstairs in the kitchen.

'Apparently Robbie heard us quarrelling the evening I was late back,' Gray told Sarah when she asked him if the police had been able to discover from him why he had run away. She herself had been reluctant to question him too much, especially since he was in such a distressed and exhausted state.

'He wanted to be with you, apparently, and so while I was downstairs he got dressed and left the house. Only he got lost and couldn't find his way in the dark, and then he became very frightened. When he found the disused hut he went inside it, and he must have fallen asleep there. I thought I was making some headway with him. I thought he was beginning to get over his dislike of me.' He sounded so anguished that Sarah's throat closed up with emotion. She ached to be able to open her arms to him as she had done to Robbie. To hold and comfort him as tenderly as she had done his child. Never had they seemed so alike... so vulnerable, and she had to forcibly remind herself that the security of her arms, her love, was the last thing that he needed or wanted.

'Things can't go on like this,' she heard him saying grimly. 'I had hoped that Robbie was beginning to settle down, to accept me as his father, but now... He needs and wants you in his life more than he does me.'

Sarah's heart jumped with guilt and pain for him.

'He's very young,' she told him. 'And don't forget he's not really used to men. He's been brought up surrounded by women, and his mother——'

'His mother taught him almost from the day he was born to hate and fear me, and I haven't helped matters, have I? I've been so damned afraid of swamping him...of oppressing him by my emotions and my needs, that I've held back...hoping that he would eventually come to me, but instead...'

'He needs time to adjust...to grow more accustomed to you,' Sarah tried to comfort him.

'Does he?' Gray's mouth twisted. 'I think we both know that's not true. "Give me a child until he is seven"—isn't that what the Jesuits used to say?' His mouth twisted again. 'I can't undo all his mother's indoctrination. Robbie will never truly I...'

He stopped, shaking his head, leaving Sarah to say softly to him, 'You're wrong, you know. I think he *does* love you, but he's so very young and so very confused, and you've got to remember that he still believes that you don't love *him*.'

'*I* don't love *him*? Of course I love him,' Gray told her thickly. 'He's my son, dammit...my child.'

'Not all parents love their children,' Sarah pointed out sadly. 'Your own wife...his mother...'

Yes, he loved him, Sarah recognised, aching with pity for him, but he could not show it, could not physically demonstrate to Robbie how much he

meant to him, and so he held himself aloof from
the little boy, through a fear that, once he allowed
Robbie to see how much he did care, his emotions
would get out of control, and that he would swamp
Robbie with a love the little boy did not want.

'Perhaps if you were to show him how much you
love him,' she suggested gently now. 'Instead of
holding aloof from him...'

Immediately Gray shook his head, barely allowing her to finish before telling her gratingly, 'I've
already told you, he doesn't want my love. Do you
know what he told them when the police found
him? He told them he hated me and that he wanted
to be with you. That he didn't want to live with me
because I had sent you away. He told them that he
wished I was the one who was dead and not his
mother.'

A huge lump of compassion blocked her throat,
making her voice sound thick and raw when she
told him, 'He's a little boy...that's all. He's attached himself to me because I'm a woman. He's
been brought up by women. Women find it easier
to show their emotions, to let down their guard.'

'Do they?'

The look he gave her made the colour rise up
under her skin as she remembered just how much
she had let down her guard in just what kind of
circumstances. She had never in her wildest imaginings believed she could be capable of such sensuality, such eroticism. She gave a tiny shiver. She
had tried desperately to dismiss such memories from
her mind, to wipe her brain clear of them, to forget
that they had ever happened, knowing that Gray
must have already dismissed them from his

memory; that to him their intimacy had simply been a male expression of helpless impotence and anger... a driven need to push away his fear for his child, to occupy his thoughts and his body with something, anything that would hold at bay the trauma of what he was going through.

'I'd better go up and check on Robbie,' she told him shakily, knowing she was using Robbie as an excuse to escape from him, and knowing from the look in his eyes that he knew it too.

CHAPTER NINE

'WE NEED to talk.'

The abrupt comment made Sarah tense and put down the mug of coffee she had just raised to her lips.

It was eight o'clock and she had just put Robbie to bed, and had been about to suggest to Gray that it was time she left.

So far Robbie was recovering surprisingly quickly from his ordeal. He had woken up during the afternoon, and, although he had not mentioned what had happened and had clung physically as well as emotionally to her, Sarah had been able to question him gently about why he had run away.

As he had told the police, he had overheard her argument with Gray and had decided that if she was not coming back then he was not going to stay with his father without her. She had told him quietly then how much his daddy loved him and how worried he had been. She had told him as well that sometimes grown-ups quarrel with one another, and he had seemed to accept what she had told him, although she couldn't help but notice the way he avoided any kind of contact with Gray.

Now, as she waited, Gray told her curtly, 'Robbie needs *you* here more than he needs me. I know you've already said that you aren't prepared to live in, but I was wondering if you might reconsider that decision and move in here.'

What could she say? She ached to refuse but she
sensed that he was in no mood to listen to her, and
as for her reminding him that they had already decided that he should find someone else to care for
Robbie... How could she do that now?

As always her soft heart was her undoing... and
besides, if she was honest with herself, didn't half
of her actually want to stay? Even when doing so
meant that she would enmesh herself even further
in the web of heartache she was tangling round
herself? Was that really what she wanted? She was
already far too emotionally involved with Robbie
as it was. And as for her feeling for Gray himself...
How could she live here in the same house with him
now, after what had happened, and yet, for
Robbie's sake, how could she not do so? She took
a deep breath, firmly pushing her own feelings to
one side, telling herself that Robbie's needs must
come first now.

'I don't want to put any kind of emotional
pressure on you,' she could hear Gray saying rawly.
'But for Robbie's sake...'

'For Robbie's sake, I'll stay,' Sarah told him, 'but
on one condition: *you* must make time for
Robbie... time to get to know him and for him to
get to know you.' He was about to speak but she
wouldn't let him, quickly overriding him, determined to make her point now before she lost her
courage and with it the ability to make him see how
important it was that the gulf between Robbie and
himself was bridged, and quickly.

'I know you're going to say you're too busy to
take time off work but that's exactly what you must
do. You *must* put Robbie first. We both must.'

There was a taut silence. She knew she was
holding her breath, half waiting for him to deny
the truth of what she was saying, to reject her plea,
but instead, to her relief, he said harshly, 'I take it
if I don't agree you'll refuse to stay—is that what
you're saying?'

She was tempted to agree, but her conscience
wouldn't let her, and so instead she shook her head,
telling him, 'No, I can't do that... but you must
see how important it is now for you to establish
contact with Robbie, and the only way you can do
that is by spending time with him. Can't you see it
isn't enough for you to tell *me* that you love him?
You have to *show* Robbie that you do. You have
to win his confidence... his trust.'

There was a long pause. She held her breath and
then heard him saying reluctantly, 'Very well, then.
I'll have to go into the office tomorrow to sort out
one or two things... but only for tomorrow. Any
urgent things that crop up I suppose I could always
deal with from here.'

He was as good as his word, and almost a week
after Robbie had terrified them both by running
away Sarah found herself holding her breath in
tense delight one morning when Robbie actually
addressed a question to his father instead of routing
it through her.

True, it was only a simple request to know how
they were going to spend the day, but it was a
breakthrough, an acknowledgement on Robbie's
part that his father existed and had a part in his
life, and she could tell from one swift look at Gray's
face that he was aware of its importance too.

The morning brought another welcome relief, when she discovered that there was no risk of her having conceived Gray's child. At least, she *told* herself that it was a relief and tried to bolster that view by reminding herself of all the reasons why she could not possibly have allowed herself to feel the slightest pleasure in the discovery that she was pregnant, and yet at the back of her mind all the time lay a small, aching pain, a small, desolate awareness of how much she would have liked to have had his child, another Robbie... or perhaps a Roberta. The thought made her smile painfully to herself. A son or a daughter, her child's sex would not have been important to her... what would have been important was that she would have been carrying Gray's child... and even though she knew he would not have wanted it... *she* would have done so.

When she went downstairs and found Robbie asking his father if they could have lunch at McDonald's the desolation that swept her filled her eyes with tears and made her womb literally ache with emptiness as she acknowledged that, if she could not have Gray's child, she would probably never have a child at all, because no man could ever mean to her what he did, and the thought of sharing with another man the intimacy she had shared with him, even though she knew that intimacy meant absolutely nothing whatsoever to him, was almost sacrilege.

She was determined that no one but she would ever know just what it was costing her to put her own feelings on one side and to stay here in the same house with Gray, acutely conscious of the way he avoided coming too close to her, the way he avoided even looking at her sometimes, almost as though... As though what? He was filled with such acute distaste and embarrassment at the memory of their shared intimacy that now her physical presence was something he had to force himself to endure for Robbie's sake?

Some days her nerves were so on edge and she was so completely conscious of him, ached so much inside for him, that she barely knew how she was going to stand it, and yet somehow or other she always did ... always managed to remind herself of why she was here, and of how important it was for Robbie's sake that they presented a harmonious and united front.

And at the same time she was aware of how difficult Gray was finding things. Sometimes the look in his eyes when he watched Robbie and was unaware of *her* watching *him* brought her close to tears of compassion for him. How could she ever have doubted how much he loved his son? She just wished she had the power to wave a magic wand and somehow or other remove all the barriers between them. Robbie was such a naturally affectionate and loving little boy, but his ability to place his trust in his father had been so damaged by his mother that, for every step forward they made, he sometimes seemed to take two back. Like the day Gray took them out for a drive and then on to a country park for a walk when Robbie refused to walk alongside his father, instead demanding that he and Sarah should walk along together while Gray walked alone behind them.

But they *were* making progress, Sarah assured herself. Last night Gray had read Robbie's bedtime story to him on his own, and now here was Robbie actually beginning to talk directly with his father.

It was no wonder Gray looked so strained and tense, though. Loving Robbie the way he did, he must be under an almost unendurable pressure.

And yet she was convinced that, given time, Robbie *would* turn to his father, would overcome his deeply ingrained mistrust of him and come to recognise Gray's love for him. And once he did her role here would be finished, her presence no longer needed, and how was she going to feel about that? How was she going to feel when she had to leave?

Like Eve locked out of Paradise? A strange kind of paradise that reduced her to desolation and the solace of the tears she wept every night in her sleep; the ache of longing and love that ceaselessly tormented her, the way she longed to be able to turn to Gray and to see reflected in his eyes all that she knew was in her own heart.

Such impossible, idiotic dreams. Why on earth did she cling to them so ridiculously when she knew that they could only add to her pain and despair?

That night, after he had had his bath and Sarah was tucking him up in bed, when she kissed him goodnight Robbie clung tightly to her and told her, 'I wish you were my mummy, Sarah.'

Tears filled her eyes and she had to turn her head away so that he wouldn't see them, but as she did so she froze.

Gray was standing just inside the bedroom door, and she knew from the look on his face that he had overheard Robbie's comment.

For a moment he just stood there, looking at her, and then silently, without a word, he turned on his heel and walked away.

'Is Daddy coming to read my story tonight?' Robbie asked her chattily, but for once this sign that he was at last coming to accept Gray's role in his life failed to lift her spirits.

'I expect so,' she responded automatically, getting up from beside the bed and heading for the door.

When she went downstairs there was no sign of Gray in the kitchen, but when she went back into the hall she could see a light shining under his study door.

She knocked on the door, and then when Gray opened it she told him quickly, unable to bring herself to look directly at him, 'Robbie's waiting for you to read to him.'

She walked away without waiting for a response, too embarrassed and too aware of how he must have felt on hearing Robbie's artless comment to be able to remain where she was.

She already knew how little he wanted her in his life and that he only tolerated her presence in his home for Robbie's sake. She had seen the way he reacted to her too often to be under any illusions there.

Whenever, by accident, she had come into any kind of close physical proximity to him he had immediately stepped back from her, had immediately reacted to her presence by distancing himself from her physically, just as he had distanced himself from her emotionally after they had made love—no, not made love...after they had had sex. She shuddered in grim distaste but refused to allow herself to alter the description, just as she had all along refused to allow herself the palliative of deceiving herself about just how little what had happened had meant to him.

She heard him going upstairs, but stayed where she was in the kitchen, expecting that when he came down again he would go straight back into the study. They might be sharing the same house, but once Robbie was in bed at night they remained strictly segregated...she either in the kitchen or in her own bedroom, Gray usually working in his study.

She was busy pretending to read an article in a newspaper when she heard him coming back downstairs, her body tensing as she waited for the now familiar sound of the study door opening and then closing again, the symbolic withdrawal from her that shut her out of his life and kept the barriers firmly in place between them.

In fact, so sure was she that he would return to his study that when instead he walked into the kitchen she was too shocked to do anything other than stare at him.

'I'm...I'm going away for a few days,' he told her abruptly. 'It's...it's business, something that can't be avoided, I'm afraid.'

What could she say? What could she do? Remind him of his promise when she had agreed to live in...remind him of how important it was that he gave Robbie his time and attention?

She opened her mouth to do so and then closed it again, knowing already that she was wasting her time. How could he do this? she wondered sadly and half angrily. How could he turn his back on Robbie like this just when the little boy was starting to lose his fear of him?

'Is it really necessary?' was all she could bring herself to say, her voice terse, betraying all that she was not saying.

A dark ridge of colour burnt along his cheekbones.

'Yes, it is,' he told her curtly. But he was avoiding looking at her and she sensed that he was withholding something from her...that he was not being entirely honest with her.

'I'll be leaving first thing in the morning.'

Sarah's mouth compressed, but before she could say anything he shocked her by telling her, 'I've already explained things to Robbie. I think he understands. I'll be gone about a month.'

A month. She swallowed back her shock and distress, too stunned to protest that he could not leave her solely in charge of Robbie for that length of time.

Later that night as she prepared for bed Sarah found herself wishing bitterly that *she* could understand as he had claimed Robbie had done. He had *promised* her that he would put Robbie first; that he would concentrate on building up the little boy's trust...and she had always felt that he was the kind of man who, once his word was given, would never go back on it, especially not for material gain. She knew how strongly he felt about his responsibility to his workforce, but surely in this instance Robbie had to come first.

And to calmly announce that he would be gone for a full month... But no, he had not been calm, she recognised with hindsight; in fact, he had been extremely tense and on edge. But *why... why* leave Robbie now, just when the little boy was starting to reach out to him?

She wished she had the courage, the confidence to put such questions to him, but knew that she did not... not even for Robbie's sake, much as she had come to love the little boy.

She swallowed hard, reliving that painful moment when Robbie had told her he wished she were his mother and the even more painful moment when she had turned her head and had known that Gray had overhead his son's comment.

Was it because of that... because he feared that she...? That she what? That she might try to use Robbie's dependence on her to...?

Tears blurred her eyes. Surely he couldn't have such a low opinion of her? Surely the fact that she had never once referred to what had happened between them the day of Robbie's disappearance *must* have shown him that she was aware of how unimportant it had been to him... or how little he would want to be reminded of it?

When at last she drifted into an exhausted sleep there were tear-stains on her face, and her heart ached with the pain of loving Gray and knowing that he would never love her in return.

When she got downstairs in the morning he had gone. There was a terse note for her, apologising

for his abrupt departure, and thanking her for all
she had done and was doing for Robbie.

For Robbie there was also a note, a touching little
gesture which the Gray she had first known would
surely never have made, and over breakfast, despite her own pain, she kept on bringing Gray into
the conversation, determined to build on the bond
that was already tentatively growing between father
and son.

She had her reward later in the day when Robbie
exclaimed, 'I wish Daddy were here, don't you,
Sarah?'

She forced herself to smile, while saying nothing.
What was there to say that Robbie, as a child, could
possibly understand?

She was already dreadfully afraid that Gray
himself had guessed how she felt about him. She
was quite certain that Sally and Ross had, even
though neither of them had said a word to her about
the situation.

A week passed without any word from Gray. Not
that she *had* expected to hear from him, Sarah told
herself, but still, he might have sent Robbie a card
from wherever it was he had gone on this oh, so
important business that would not keep.

She had been sleeping badly, dragging herself
through the days in a state of inertia and misery,
forcing herself to make an effort for Robbie's sake,
acknowledging now just how much comfort she had
derived merely from Gray's presence in the house,
even though at the same time she had been forced
to endure her awareness of his physical distancing
of himself from her, as though he could hardly bear
sometimes to be in the same room with her.

She had put Robbie to bed; the house was clean; there was nothing really for her to do...nothing to occupy her other than the book she had bought while out shopping. She switched on the television in the sitting-room, and told herself that once she had watched the news she might as well go straight to bed, but the long days of loneliness and despair had taken their toll on her, and long before it was time for the evening's news programme she had fallen asleep where she was.

Letting himself into the house half an hour later, Gray found her curled up in a chair in the sitting-room, looking more like a little girl than a woman, with her hair in a pony-tail and her face free of make-up.

An aching wave of longing swept him as he stood watching her. He had left because he could no longer endure the agony of living in such proximity to her, and now he was back because he could no longer endure the agony of living without her.

Pain if he stayed, pain if he left. He grimaced to himself. There was no panacea for his love for her, as she had made it plain enough the day he had lost his head, lost all control, and had been idiotic enough to give in to his intense need and love for her, driven by his fear for Robbie to give in to his feelings, his need in the most primitive and passionate way there was. He could never forgive himself for that...never.

She stirred in her sleep. He was about to move away, but before he could do so she opened her eyes.

'Gray.'

Sarah couldn't believe her eyes.

Her heart was beating far, far too fast, her voice husky with emotion as she stared hungrily at him, absorbing the sight of him, the knowledge that his presence was an actual reality and not merely some by-product of her over-active imagination.

How many times had she sat here in the evening, tormenting herself by fantasising about him walking in, coming to her, taking her in his arms and...?

Quickly she pulled her thoughts back to reality.

'But you said you'd be gone for a month.'

'Yes.' His voice was terse and tense as though he was having to fight for self-control.

She focused fully on him, shocked by the realisation that he had lost weight, his skin taut over his cheekbones, the normal sharp intensity of his eyes softened and blurred as though he was under considerable emotional strain.

'I couldn't stay away any longer.' The words seemed to be dragged from him as though they were a bitter acknowledgement of some kind of failure.

For a moment she couldn't make any response, too aware of his own tension to be able to react, and then she realised what he was saying and there was joy as well as compassion in her voice as she guessed softly, 'You missed Robbie.'

'Robbie?' He stared at her and then told her on a groan, 'Yes, yes, I missed Robbie, but not one tenth as much as I missed you. Oh, God, Sarah, I shouldn't be saying this to you, shouldn't be laying this burden on you, after all the other burdens I've already laid on you, but coming in here, seeing you lying there... remembering how it felt to hold you in my arms, to touch your body, to feel it responding to mine...

'After Angela I swore I'd never let a woman get close to me again; that I'd never put myself in the position of being emotionally vulnerable; that sex was something I'd rather live without than take the risk of admitting into my life, either as a physical appetite that needed appeasing or as part of a package that carried the added dangers of emotional and mental bonding with someone who might one day change her mind and walk out on me, and I thought I'd succeeded. I certainly told myself that I was happier without a woman in my life than I had been married to someone I neither loved nor respected, even if I had once believed I loved her.

'And then I met you. From the first moment I saw you sitting there under the willow with Robbie...my son...the two of you staring at me with dislike and fear in your eyes, I knew that all I'd told myself, all the rules I'd made for myself, meant nothing.

'Even then the temptation to just take hold of you and go on holding you was so intense... I'd never experienced anything like it. I'd never wanted to experience anything like it. I told myself it was just a freak of emotional responsiveness to the problems I was having with Robbie, but I knew in my heart I was just searching desperately for something I could use to stave off the truth. I knew then that what I felt for you was a whole world away from the immature choice I'd made for Robbie's mother.

'Long before the second time Robbie went missing I'd stopped trying to fool myself. I knew that I loved you, and that I would love you for the rest of my life. I hated myself for that weakness, and sometimes I hated you as well for causing it. I can't ask for your forgiveness for what I did... those memories are too precious to me. Just to be able to hold you... to touch you... I swear I never intended things to get so out of control. I never intended to do anything more than just hold you, but once you *were* in my arms...' He gave a deep shudder, and Sarah, who had been listening to him in disbelieving silence, felt a shivering sensual response convulse her own body, a heated erotic awareness of him, aroused by what he was saying and what she was remembering, but she fought it down, telling herself that she must be imagining what he was saying to her; that she must be hallucinating.

'I went away for Robbie's sake, inventing urgent business that did not exist, because I knew if I stayed I'd go out of my mind with wanting you, but once I was away from you things weren't any better. I thought about you night and day, ached for you, longed for you... woke up at night with my body on fire from my dreams of you, and my arms aching to hold you.' He stopped abruptly.

'I shouldn't be telling you any of this. I never intended to tell you. I'd got it all planned. I was going to come back and tell you that I wanted you to leave; that I thought Robbie was becoming too attached to you.' He gave a bitter laugh. 'I didn't even have the guts to tell you the truth and so I was going to use Robbie as an excuse, even though I know how much he loves and needs you.

'I heard him telling you that he wishes you were his mother. God, he can't wish that more than I

wish it. I wish you *were* his mother, my wife, my
lover, my woman. I wish I could stop remembering
the way you opened your arms to me when I needed
you, the way you gave yourself to me so selflessly,
so tenderly. Sarah...'

The anguished way he said her name made her
eyes sting with tears.

She was halfway towards him when he said it
again, this time with sharply terse rejection that
made her stop to focus on his taut face.

'No, don't come any closer,' he begged her rawly.
'If you do...'

It gave her all the courage she needed, ignoring
her fear, her self-consciousness, holding firmly on
to what she had heard him saying. She walked determinedly towards him, asking shakily, 'If I do,
you'll what, Gray?'

She was close enough to him now for her breath
to brush his mouth, for her senses to pick up on
the rapid thud of his heartbeat, the stormy
emotional arousal darkening his eyes, the warm
male scent of him that made her nerve-endings
quiver.

'I'll...' He stopped, groaning her name as she
looked at his mouth, refusing to hide any longer
how she felt about him. In the split-second it took
for her to lift her gaze from his mouth to his eyes
her own mouth started to tremble and so did her
body.

His arms were wrapped around her, his mouth
devouring hers, his kiss so possessively rough that
it almost hurt, but she welcomed the slight pain
because it reinforced the reality of what was happening. This was no practised seductive kiss; this

was the kiss of a man held in the grip of such a deep and strong emotion that he was beyond the limits of his own self-control, and she gave herself up to it, welcoming the harshly guttural sounds he made in his throat and the pressure of his hands as they swept over her body, moulding and caressing it as though he could hardly believe that she was actually real.

When his hands touched her breasts they both trembled. The ache inside her body made her cling dizzily to him, returning the words of love he was muttering into her ear and against her skin, letting the joy building up inside her have its head so that she was euphoric with the intensity of learning that he loved her.

'I want you. I want you so much,' Gray was telling her hoarsely as he cupped her face and kissed her. 'But not yet, not until I've convinced you that I love you...not until you've told me that you forgive me for treating you so badly...not until you convince me that this isn't all a dream and that I'm going to wake up and find myself miles away and with my arms empty. You do love me, don't you, Sarah? This isn't just because you feel sorry for me? I know how tender and compassionate you are, how you hate to see anyone hurting.'

'I love you.'

Her voice shook a little as she made the admission, but her apprehension turned to tremulous excitement and awareness when he started to kiss her, her body responding joyously to his touch, to its knowledge of his love and desire.

Wrapped in one another's arms, neither of them heard the study door open, until Robbie demanded curiously, 'Daddy, why are you kissing Sarah?'

'Why? Because she's going to marry me and be your mummy, that's why. At least, I hope she's going to marry me,' Gray murmured seriously as he held her slightly away from him and looked down into her eyes.

There was just enough insecurity, just enough tormenting self-doubt and fear in his eyes to remind her of Robbie at his most vulnerable. Closing the gap between them, she bent down and took hold of Robbie's hand with one of her own, her voice soft with love as she assured him, 'I'd love to marry you, Gray. There is one condition, though.'

She felt the tension grip him, and knew what he must be thinking. Robbie's mother had once imposed conditions on him, but Robbie's mother was a ghost she intended to banish completely from their lives.

'What condition?' he demanded harshly.

Against his mouth, ignoring the tension she could feel in his body, she whispered, 'I don't want Robbie to be an only child. I want you, I want your love and I want your children, Gray.'

'The first two you've already got, and as for the third... I agree with you, Robbie needs brothers and sisters. However, right now what Robbie needs more than anything else is to be securely tucked up in his own bed, fast asleep.'

The look he was giving her made her blush and laugh, but she didn't argue when Gray picked Robbie up in his arms and headed for the door with him. Soon she would be the one Gray was holding in his arms...soon he would be holding her, touching her, loving her. He had paused by the door and she saw from the look he gave her that he knew what was going through her mind and that he shared her need and her love.

Over Robbie's head he mouthed silently to her, 'I love you,' and then, as though unable to stop himself, still carrying Robbie, he came back to her, kissing her gently on the lips and then more lingeringly until Robbie protested sleepily that he was getting squashed.

'Soon. I'll be back soon,' he promised her as he carried Robbie towards the door.

POSTCARDS FROM EUROPE

HARLEQUIN PRESENTS®

Hi!
I can't believe that I'm living on Cyprus—home of Aphrodite, the legendary goddess of love——or that I'm suddenly the owner of a five-star hotel.

Nikolaos Konstantin obviously can't quite believe any of it, either!

Love, Emily

Harlequin® Historical

LOOK TO THE PAST FOR FUTURE FUN AND EXCITEMENT!

The past the Harlequin Historical way, that is. 1994 is going to be a banner year for us, so here's a preview of what to expect:

* The continuation of our bigger book program, with titles such as *Across Time* by Nina Beaumont, *Defy the Eagle* by Lynn Bartlett and *Unicorn Bride* by Claire Delacroix.

* A 1994 March Madness promotion featuring four titles by promising new authors Gayle Wilson, Cheryl St. John, Madris Dupree and Emily French.

* Brand-new in-line series: DESTINY'S WOMEN by Merline Lovelace and HIGHLANDER by Ruth Langan; and new chapters in old favorites, such as the SPARHAWK saga by Miranda Jarrett and the WARRIOR series by Margaret Moore.

* *Promised Brides,* an exciting brand-new anthology with stories by Mary Jo Putney, Kristin James and Julie Tetel.

* Our perennial favorite, the Christmas anthology, this year featuring Patricia Gardner Evans, Kathleen Eagle, Elaine Barbieri and Margaret Moore.

Watch for these programs and titles wherever Harlequin Historicals are sold.

HARLEQUIN HISTORICALS... A TOUCH OF MAGIC!

HHPROMO94

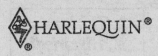

Harlequin Books requests the pleasure of your company this June in Eternity, Massachusetts, for WEDDINGS, INC.

For generations, couples have been coming to Eternity, Massachusetts, to exchange wedding vows. Legend has it that those married in Eternity's chapel are destined for a lifetime of happiness. And the residents are more than willing to give the legend a hand.

Beginning in June, you can experience the legend of Eternity. Watch for one title per month, across all of the Harlequin series.

HARLEQUIN BOOKS... NOT THE SAME OLD STORY!

HARLEQUIN®

PRESENTS Plus

Nathan Parnell needs a wife and mother for his young son. Sasha Redford and her daughter need a home. It's a match made in heaven, although no one's discussed the small matter of love.

Emily Musgrave and her nephew are on the run. But has she compounded her problems by accepting the help of Sandy McPherson, a total stranger?

Fall in love with Nathan and Sandy—Sasha and Emily do!

Watch for

In Need of a Wife by Emma Darcy
Harlequin Presents Plus #1679

and

Catch Me If You Can by Anne McAllister
Harlequin Presents Plus #1680

Harlequin Presents Plus
The best has just gotten better!

Available in September wherever Harlequin books are sold.

HARLEQUIN®

Don't miss these Harlequin favorites by some of our most
distinguished authors!
And now you can receive a discount by ordering two or more titles!

HT #25525	THE PERFECT HUSBAND by Kristine Rolofson	$2.99	☐
HT #25554	LOVERS' SECRETS by Glenda Sanders	$2.99	☐
HP #11577	THE STONE PRINCESS by Robyn Donald	$2.99	☐
HP #11554	SECRET ADMIRER by Susan Napier	$2.99	☐
HR #03277	THE LADY AND THE TOMCAT by Bethany Campbell	$2.99	☐
HR #03283	FOREIGN AFFAIR by Eva Rutland	$2.99	☐
HS #70529	KEEPING CHRISTMAS by Marisa Carroll	$3.39	☐
HS #70578	THE LAST BUCCANEER by Lynn Erickson	$3.50	☐
HI #22256	THRICE FAMILIAR by Caroline Burnes	$2.99	☐
HI #22238	PRESUMED GUILTY by Tess Gerritsen	$2.99	☐
HAR #16496	OH, YOU BEAUTIFUL DOLL by Judith Arnold	$3.50	☐
HAR #16510	WED AGAIN by Elda Minger	$3.50	☐
HH #28719	RACHEL by Lynda Trent	$3.99	☐
HH #28795	PIECES OF SKY by Marianne Willman	$3.99	☐

Harlequin Promotional Titles

#97122	LINGERING SHADOWS by Penny Jordan	$5.99	☐
	(limited quantities available on certain titles)		

	AMOUNT	$
DEDUCT:	**10% DISCOUNT FOR 2+ BOOKS**	$
	POSTAGE & HANDLING	$
	($1.00 for one book, 50¢ for each additional)	
	APPLICABLE TAXES*	$
	TOTAL PAYABLE	$
	(check or money order—please do not send cash)	

To order, complete this form and send it, along with a check or money order for the
total above, payable to Harlequin Books, to: **In the U.S.:** 3010 Walden Avenue,
P.O. Box 9047, Buffalo, NY 14269-9047; **In Canada:** P.O. Box 613, Fort Erie, Ontario,
L2A 5X3.

Name: _____

Address:_____City: _____

State/Prov.: _____ Zip/Postal Code: _____

*New York residents remit applicable sales taxes.
 Canadian residents remit applicable GST and provincial taxes..

HBACK-JS